DUST ROAD

TOM HUDDLESTON

nosy crow

First published in the UK in 2020 by Nosy Crow Ltd
The Crow's Nest, 14 Baden Place
Crosby Row, London, SE1 1YW

Nosy Crow and associated logos are trademarks and/or registered
trademarks of Nosy Crow Ltd

A CIP catalogue record for this book is available from the
British Library.

Printed and bound in Great Britain by Clays Ltd, Elcograf S.p.A.
Typeset by Tiger Media

Papers used by Nosy Crow are made from wood grown in
sustainable forests

ISBN: 978 1 78800 648 4

www.nosycrow.com

DUST ROAD

Also by
Tom Huddleston

For Rosie,
my travelling partner
and my destination

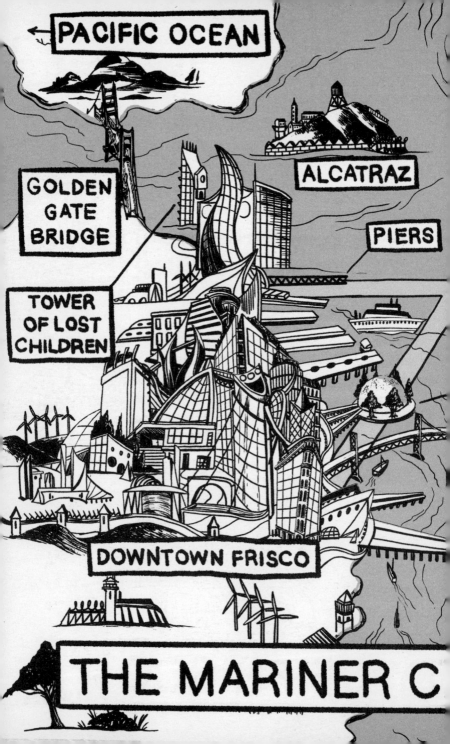

Prologue

The car's engine growled like an animal on the hunt, painted steel gleaming beneath the crescent moon. Lynx shifted gears as stone buildings rose on either side, their roofs broken open to the sky. Empty doorways were heaped with rubble and the rusted shells of vehicles lay peeling on the cracked tarmac street. A hot wind blew, and through the open window Lynx could taste dust and desert sand, and just the faintest salt tang of the sea. They would soon run out of road.

Brick dust ground beneath the wheels as the car skidded into a turn, the motorbike up ahead leaning so steeply that its rider's knee almost scraped the ground. Lynx's lip curled with satisfaction. It wouldn't be long now. The Wildcats would run their quarry down and haul her in for justice.

Lynx's car was painted the same mottled black-and-dun as the desert cat that had inspired its owner's name. It was a low-slung speedster pounded together from the scavenged parts of other vehicles, custom-built for speed and raw power. It had a snarling mouth scrawled across the front grille and gleaming eyes on the headlamps. Its throttle barked like a wild thing.

Hearing the screech of brakes, Lynx glanced in the rear-view mirror and saw the others following. Leo's vehicle was big, a hulking mass of gold-sprayed steel topped with a mane of rusted metal mesh. The sandy-haired boy hunkered low behind the dashboard, slamming the stick forward, high wheels jouncing over piles of strewn stone. Behind him came Tigress, her night-black car streaked with blazing orange stripes. She overtook Leo on the inside, grinning through sharpened fangs as she scraped past his front bumper and swung in behind Lynx.

But Lynx didn't smile. This was no time for games. If they allowed the traitor to escape, their bosses would not forgive them. And as group leader it was Lynx's responsibility to ensure that things went smoothly, that the woman up ahead on the silver motorbike was run down and brought back. The Wildcats' reputation, their growing notoriety as the most dangerous pack of road hogs this side of the Rockies – all of it was on the line.

Then Lynx heard a sound and felt a thin shiver of glee. It was a low rushing roar, steady and close. The wind blew stronger, cooler, as the buildings opened out to reveal nothing beyond, nothing but the high moon and the distant stars, and the glittering black expanse of the sea.

The bike slowed, the rider's helmeted head jerking anxiously from left to right. She's taken a wrong turn, Lynx thought. She's backed herself into a corner. And she knows it.

The biker twisted the throttle as she turned north, following the tumbledown seafront. The road was old concrete, parts of it subsiding into the risen ocean. The bike weaved smoothly around these open sinkholes but Lynx was forced to slow the car, feeling the way forward. Leo leaned on the horn and Lynx made a rude gesture, sure it could be seen through the rear windscreen.

The motorbike was heading for a long steel pier that branched from the waterfront and out into the dark waters of the Gulf. Beyond it a flickering orange haze lit the horizon, low clouds reflecting the glow from the old city of Houston. The city itself was broken now, an empty, flooded ruin. But The Five had rekindled the oil refineries north of town, their flames burning day and night, their generators gleaming against the dark. To

Lynx it was almost magical, an echo of the days when the whole skyline would've been lit up like the sun. Before civilisation fell, and the continent went dark.

The bike turned on to the pier and Lynx could hear boards rattling under its wheels. What was the traitor doing? She'd intentionally put herself at the Wildcats' mercy, with nowhere left to go. Lynx weaved around the last of the potholes and followed her on to the pier, where steel struts groaned and the weather-worn hulks of old burger stands and amusement arcades framed the wide wooden walkway. Clowns and elephants watched with flaking eyes as the Wildcats fanned out, blocking any chance of escape. But the motorbike had stopped, its rider twisting to face them. She removed her helmet, glanced briefly at the comwatch on her wrist, then held up a hand.

"That's far enough," she called, her face pale in the moonlight. On her back Lynx could see a bulging canvas pack, stuffed with all the contraband medicine she'd taken from The Five's stores. "You've got me."

The three vehicles slowed and Lynx scanned the circular platform at the end of the pier. There appeared to be no other exit, no hidden walkway or stairs. The only way out was the way they'd come. The Wildcats slid to a halt, switching off their engines to conserve gasoline. For a moment all was silent, just the lapping of the waves and the tick of cooling metal.

Then Lynx unbelted and opened the door, straightening with one hand on the roof. The traitor watched with dark eyes. "You ran me down," she said. "I thought you would."

Lynx frowned. "Did you honestly imagine you could get away clean? You must think we're dumb as a box of rocks, us and The Five."

The thief shook her head. "Not dumb," she said. "Just … busy. The Five are overstretching themselves, Lynx. Between the pill factory and the refinery and the farms, not to mention this crazy scheme about bringing the states together… It felt like a good time to get out. I only took enough to help me get started."

"People rely on those meds," Tigress put in. "Insulin and antibiotics – those are lives you're playing with."

The woman snorted. "Come on, you don't care about that, and neither do The Five. They care about profit, and they care about power. They just want to be in charge, to tell people like us what to do. Well, not me. I don't need those freaks telling me what I—"

"Hey," Leo barked, slamming his door. "We don't use that word."

The thief's face broke into a smile. "Freaks? What other

word is there? I don't know why they are like they are, but Brad, you know as well as I do that it ain't natural."

The boy's face flushed. "Leo," he growled. "My name's Leo now."

She snorted. "Oh right, I forgot. Sorry, pussycat."

"Quiet," Lynx snapped. "The Five told us to bring you back. They didn't say in how many pieces."

The thief laughed. "I'm sorry, I just… I know you think you're tough, and there are probably a few folks out there who are actually scared of you. But when I look at you, I just see three kids. Three kids with ridiculous hair and stupid names who, one of these days, are going to get themselves in way more trouble than they can handle."

"Shut your mouth!" Leo snarled. "We're the Wildcats – what are you?"

The thief glanced at her watch, and back towards the sea. Then she shrugged, smiled and winked at them. "I'm leaving," she said, replacing her helmet and firing up the bike.

Lynx cursed and dropped back into the car, turning the key. The motorbike was already moving, gunning towards Leo just as his engine rumbled into life. There was a space between the cars that the bike might just slip through, but Lynx knew it was pointless; the Wildcats were still faster, and there were three of them.

Then something unexpected happened. The bike twisted again, wheels squealing as it made a sharp spin in the centre of the platform. Lynx watched open-mouthed as the thief hit the throttle, making straight for the end of the pier. There was a gap in the rusty railing and the traitor aimed for it, seemingly determined to throw herself headlong into the ocean. The bike cleared the pier and shot out into open air, wheels spinning furiously.

Then over the rush of the sea Lynx heard another sound, the low moan of a foghorn. Leo had already jumped from his car, sprinting to the railing and looking down in disbelief. Lynx joined him, gripping the cold steel with both hands.

A battered fishing boat chugged from the shadow of the pier, waves slapping against her hull. The motorbike lay on its side in a tangle of green nets, the woman sprawled beside it on the deck. As they watched she picked herself up, raising a hand as the boat rumbled away into the dark.

Lynx pounded on the railing so hard it hurt. "I should've seen that coming."

"Yes, you should."

The dark-haired man crouched, frowning coldly. The scar above his right eye gleamed in the low electric light. Behind him on the wall was a huge, featureless painting, black like the mouth of a cave.

"You should've guessed she'd have a plan," the second man added.

"You should've anticipated her moves," said the third.

"Instead you let her make a fool of you," the fourth added.

"You let her make a fool of *us*," the fifth finished bitterly.

Lynx wanted to protest, but what was the point? The Five were right, as always. The thief had escaped and the Wildcats had been powerless to stop her.

The black-suited brothers took their seats, the long table framed by painted slabs of pure darkness. Even after three years, Lynx could barely tell the men apart – one had a scar above his eye, another a few grey hairs, but in all important respects The Five were completely identical. And that was precisely as it should be – they were united, unassailable, they wore one face and spoke with one voice. They were the ultimate power in the city of Houston and far beyond.

"We're good to you, aren't we?" One leaned forward, his face gleaming like polished plastic.

"We feed you," one of his brothers chimed in.

"We clothe you," added another.

"We give you our trust."

"We don't question your … lifestyle."

8

Lynx flushed, but it was true. The Five's support had never wavered, even when the girl who had been their best driver had come to the realisation that they weren't a girl any more.

"We encourage you to be whoever you need to be."

"We're on your side, no matter what."

"And all we ask in return is that you and your friends are loyal."

"That you do your best."

"And this, tonight … this doesn't feel like your best."

"Is that a fair assessment?"

Lynx nodded slowly. "Maybe, but—"

"No buts, Lynx."

"No excuses."

"There's only one thing for it."

"One way to fix this."

"Don't you agree?"

Lynx sighed. "You want me to bring her back. And the goods too."

The Five smiled in perfect unison and Lynx had to suppress a shiver. Sometimes their behaviour was so synchronised that it was downright uncanny.

"The goods aren't important."

"Or at least, they're less important."

"We want the thief."

"We have to make an example of her."

"Prove to everyone that you can't steal from The Five and get away with it."

They leaned in, their elbows on the table.

"This is an important time for us, Lynx."

"Big things are happening."

"There's going to be a gathering."

"Out in the desert."

"A great celebration."

"A grand unification."

"And we'd like you to be there."

Lynx nodded. "Sirs, I'd be honoured to—"

"But you can only come if you bring a friend."

"A guest."

"You know who."

"Of course you do."

"Find her."

"Bring her."

The first leaned in again, so close that Lynx could see nothing but his emerald eyes, flecked with gold, the white scar shining above the right one.

"Or don't come back at all."

1

The Tower

The red-brick hall was streaked with sunbeams, shimmering down through the water and illuminating the faces of beasts and men and gods. In the flooded gallery the silence was deep, just the whisper of the waves above and the soft shifting of silt and sediment on the flagstone floor.

Joe had visited many such places in recent weeks, drowned museums and sunken palaces, vast and old and elegant. He wished he'd been able to see them before the Wall broke and the water came, when these halls were full of sound and people. London had been a living city then, one of the last in the world. Now it was just like everywhere else, flooded and broken and washed away.

But there was still beauty here, if you looked at it the right way. The walls of the gallery were almost bare, stripped clean by the first salvage crews to pick through the flooded city. But a few paintings still hung in place, waterlogged beneath cracked panes of glass. Figures and landscapes bled into one another; painted eyes leaked colourful tears as drop by drop the sea absorbed them.

Shouldering his pack, Joe kicked through an empty window and angled up towards the surface. He could see the outline of the skiff overhead, a black oval surrounded by floating flotsam, the crust of rubbish and loose soil and plant matter that covered the still, brackish water inside the Wall. He broke through, spitting out his mouthpiece and taking a lungful of fresh air.

Kara sat up in the boat, rubbing her eyes and sweeping back her lank yellow hair. Joe swam towards her, objects bobbing in his face – a blue teacup, a wad of matted paper, a lump of earth with grass still clinging to it. He pushed them aside, taking hold of Kara's outstretched hand and climbing over the skiff's wooden gunwale.

"Having a nice snooze?" he asked, sipping from a bottle of chemically filtered water to wash the salty taste from his mouth. "Dreaming about how wonderful I am and how much you lurve me?"

Kara raised an eyebrow. "I was just catching up. I didn't sleep much last night."

Joe snorted. "I know. You kicked me six times." They

didn't really need to share a bed any more – they had their own place now, with two whole rooms. But they still did it, mostly out of habit. "Are you worrying about something?"

"I'm fine," Kara said, a little too quickly. "You were taking your time so I dozed off. What's so fascinating down there anyway?"

Joe looked up at the sheer face of the museum, the high brick wall throwing the skiff into shadow. He shrugged. "It's just an interesting place. A bit old and spooky, but I like it."

Kara got to her feet. "This whole City's old and spooky. And I don't like it at all."

She stood in the prow, gazing out over the filthy, encrusted water. Buildings jutted from the brine, concrete towers and church spires and chimney-topped terraces, all silent and shadowy under the shifting sky. There was no sign of any other boats or salvage teams, but that was hardly unusual. The first days following the Flood had been a free-for-all, the rescue efforts hampered by a mad scramble as looters and City refugees came in and grabbed whatever they could. But in recent months, order had been restored – the new authorities had locked London down, and now the only ones allowed to dive inside the Wall were those with an official licence and a

14

signed permit. Both of which Joe had, largely because the person the Shanties had chosen as their new prime minister happened to be his old schoolteacher, Miss Ella King.

"Well, we're not here on a sightseeing trip," Kara said, turning back. "Come on, let's see what you've got."

Joe opened his backpack, tipping out the objects he'd been sent to find – four metal sculptures, misshapen and abstract, with appendages sticking from them almost like arms.

"What are they supposed to be?" Kara asked, wrinkling her nose. "They just look like more junk."

Joe crouched, studying the bronze blobs. "I think they're sort of cool. Like, I don't know, like thoughts or something. Ideas you haven't quite finished having."

Kara rolled her eyes. "Whatever. I just don't see why our buyer would pay so much for them."

"Maybe she thinks they're cool too. Not everything's about money." Joe squinted up at her. "How much will this bring us up to, anyway? Have we saved enough for Canada?"

That had been Joe's dream for as long as he could remember – to escape the hectic floating slum they called the Shanties to a place of trees and mountains and peace and quiet.

"Not quite," Kara said without looking at him. "Soon, though."

"Maybe we should've gone with Nate," Joe mused. "It might have been fun to see where the Mariners live." The Ark *Neptune* had set sail the day before, under orders from the Mariner High Council to return to its home port of Frisco, thousands of miles away on the far coast of America. Their friend Nate had wanted them to come along, but Kara had flat-out refused.

"Fun?" she snorted now. "I've had enough of those floating loonies to last a lifetime. I know, I know, they're not all bad. But I still don't think I'm ready for a whole city full of them."

"It's just that you said we could leave the Shanties," Joe complained. "But we still haven't."

"We'll go when the time's right," Kara snapped. "Stop pestering me about it."

Joe felt a quiver of unease. Kara had always had a quick temper, if someone deserved it. But recently it seemed like she was annoyed at everyone, even Joe. He supposed it had something to do with growing up; Kara was sixteen now and he'd heard people got in funny moods at that age. Joe was still only eleven, or at least that was his best guess. His parents were the only ones who'd know for sure, and he hadn't seen them in quite a lot of years.

"Hey, that's weird," Kara said suddenly. "D'you think they're meant to be up there?"

She was gesturing across the water, between the towers to the concrete Wall on the horizon. The Wall was a perfect oval, a smooth, sheer-sided bowl enclosing the entire City. Once it had kept out the rising water but now there was a huge crack in it, a ragged cleft where the bomb placed by the Mariner terrorist Redeye had torn out the foundations. It was towards this gap that Kara was pointing, and as Joe shielded his eyes he saw dark figures up there, scaling the shattered stone.

"Maybe it's a construction crew," he mused. "Maybe Miss Ella's finally found someone mad enough to try and patch it up."

"Maybe," Kara said doubtfully. "But I don't see their boat. And what's that noise?"

Joe held his breath and listened. Beneath the lap of the waves he could hear a steady drone, growing in volume. "Sounds like a motor. A jetski or something."

"There!" Kara said, grabbing his arm. "Look!"

Facing them was a wide expanse of open water with just a few scattered buildings poking through. This had once been the path of the River Thames, Joe knew, though it had been paved over even before the Wall went up. Now along the ancient watercourse something was moving – not a boat or a jetski but a sort of bulge below the surface, travelling under its own power. It was flanked by two similar shapes, something trailing behind them in the water.

"I think Nate told me about these," Joe recalled. "The Mariners call them DPVs, diver propulsion vehicles. It's a sort of propeller that you hang on to and it pulls you through the water."

"Perfect if you don't want to be seen," Kara pointed out.

"You think they're looters?" Joe asked. "Maybe we should go back and tell someone."

"Looters with Mariner tech?" Kara wondered dubiously. "And they look like they know exactly where they're going."

Joe traced the vehicles' path, looking east along the Thames. "London Bridge is that way," he said. "And the Bank of England, but there's no money left in it." Since he'd started salvaging inside the Wall he'd become fascinated by the old city; even the names seemed to have a strange kind of magic. "And there's St Paul's, the Tower of London, the Monument, but it's all been picked c—"

"Wait, go back," Kara said. "Did you say the Tower? Isn't that where they've been keeping—"

18

"John Cortez," Joe finished, looking at her in horror. The Mariner captain had masterminded the attack on London in which thousands had died; Kara and Joe had very nearly been among them. His imprisonment in the Tower had been a symbolic act – he had all but destroyed this great city, now he languished in its most infamous jail.

"Nate always said Cortez had friends," Kara said. "A whole network of supporters, right across the globe. What if they've come to bust him out?"

Joe reached for the skiff's outboard motor. "We have to go back. We have to tell someone and—"

"And risk them getting away?" Kara asked. "Not on your life. Start her up, quiet as you can."

Joe thought about protesting but he knew it was pointless. Once Kara got an idea in her head she'd see it through, whatever the consequences. He tugged the starter cable and the engine rattled, kicking out wisps of grey smoke.

"What if they've got guns?" he asked, steering along the stone face of the gallery.

"We'll just follow them for now," Kara said. "See what they're up to, then decide what to do."

Refuse stacked against the bow as they moved into the sunlight, weaving through the line of buildings that would once have marked the south bank of the river.

But as they passed over the submerged span of London Bridge and scanned the open water beyond, Joe realised that the divers had vanished.

Kara gestured and he cut the engine. "Where did they go?" she whispered. "D'you think they saw us?"

"I don't know," Joe said. "But look, there's the Tower up ahead."

The medieval prison rose from the water, a sturdy square of grey stone ringed with crenellated battlements. Its corner turrets were topped with pale domes, tattered flags fluttering in the breeze. The outer wall was almost entirely submerged, just the top few feet rising from the waves.

"What if you're wrong?" Joe asked. "What if they're just ordinary looters? They might not be going there at all."

"Then we'll tell the guards and they can report it," Kara said. "But either way we—"

A loud *crack* sounded and something struck the boat, splinters flying from the gunwale. Kara dropped, pulling Joe down as a second bullet punched right through the hull, embedding itself in the starboard side. Water began to gulp through the hole.

"They shot at us!" Joe said. "I told you they would."

"Clever you," Kara muttered as they peered over the

side of the skiff.

The divers were some distance away, clinging to the upper branches of a leafless, sunken tree. The tallest of the three held a rifle and was loading more bullets into the chamber. One of the others gestured but the tall one ignored them, taking aim. Joe and Kara ducked as the shot passed inches overhead, thudding into a nearby building.

Then they heard motors whine as the divers dropped back into the water, activating their propellers and curving towards the Tower. Kara yanked the starter cable and the engine rumbled as she steered in pursuit.

"You're crazy," Joe protested. "Those shots were meant to scare us off!"

"They didn't work," Kara said through gritted teeth.

"But we're sinking." The water was past Joe's ankles and still pouring in. "We'll never make it."

"So we'll go as far as we can then swim," Kara said. "But I won't let them free him. I just won't."

Water splashed over the prow as the skiff picked up speed and Joe scanned the passing refuse for something to bail out with. He grabbed a plastic bowl, but it had so many holes in it that it barely made a difference.

"Look," Kara said, pointing. The three figures were climbing on to the Tower's curtain wall, wearing blue-black wetsuits with hoods and built-in breath masks. Even from this distance Joe could see they were Mariner-made.

"We're coming after you," Kara growled. "Just you w—"

The skiff tipped suddenly, water gushing over the port side. Joe snatched for his pack as the boat flipped, but he was too late to save the bronze sculptures. They sank rapidly into the black depths.

"So much for getting paid," he grumbled and Kara smiled sadly, treading water.

"I'm sorry, Joe. But this is more important."

They swam in the direction of the Tower, through a bobbing archipelago of metal cans and plastic containers. At last they reached the battlements and Joe pulled himself up, stopping to catch his breath. But Kara didn't pause, hurrying along a stone walkway towards a small, steel-roofed guard tower. Joe picked himself up and followed.

The door stood open and Kara gestured for him to stay back, peering inside. Then she beckoned to him. The guardroom was low and dark, the walls made of rough, ancient granite. But it was empty, a door on the far side standing wide.

"Where is everyone?" she asked. "Shouldn't there be someone on duty?"

"Maybe the Mariners paid them off," Joe whispered. "Or, you know, killed them."

They followed another short walkway, pushing through an arched wooden door into the main Tower. For a brief moment Joe thought the high-ceilinged room was crowded with people, all standing in silence. Then he saw that they were only dummies, plastic figures sealed in glass cases, wearing plush robes and frilly dresses and suits of steel armour. Another casket was stacked with swords and pikes and battleaxes, and Kara eyed them keenly as they passed. But to Joe's relief she left them alone, exiting the room into a long stone corridor.

Now they could hear something up ahead – a sustained hiss, like escaping steam. Kara slowed and Joe huddled behind her, creeping towards an opening at the end of the hall. Light danced on the walls and suddenly he recognised the sound for what it was: the whine of a cutting torch.

They peered into a small, enclosed antechamber. The torch was being operated by two of the wetsuited Mariners, crouching by a steel door and attempting to shear through the padlock. The third stood a little way back, the cowl of his wetsuit pulled back to reveal a shaved head and a broad, tattooed neck.

"I told you," Kara whispered to Joe, her words almost drowned by the noise of the torch. "They're trying to free Cortez. We have to stop them."

"Wait," Joe said. "That guy's twice your size – you can't—"

But Kara was already moving, keeping low as she ducked into the room. She crossed the floor in two bounds, grabbing the standing Mariner around the waist and using her weight to drag him off his feet. He landed hard and Kara straddled him, shoving him flat on his back before he could cry out. His rifle skittered away and Joe ran to grab it, hugging it to his chest. The other Mariners hadn't even glanced back – the torch was too loud and they were engrossed in their task.

Kara pinned the fallen Mariner, taking hold of his arms. But he was a big man, and strong; he broke loose and swung at her, splitting her lip. Kara's face flushed with anger as she shifted her weight, driving her fist into the man's stomach. He let out a wheezing cry but Kara hit him again, smashing his cheek, drawing blood. Then she bent double, wrapping both hands around the big man's throat and squeezing as hard as she could.

"I won't let you take him!" she hissed. "Cortez has to pay for what he—"

"Kara!" a voice cried. "Stop!"

The noise of the torch had ceased and the other Mariners had turned to see what was happening. One jumped to his feet, tugging back the hood of his wetsuit to reveal a pale face, stricken with horror.

"Nate!" Kara breathed, letting go of her victim. "What are you…? Why are you…?"

The Mariner boy held up both hands as he stepped closer. His companion put down the cutting torch and reached to her waist, tugging out a small pistol and training it on Kara.

"Nate, who are these … children?" she demanded, her eyes flicking to the rifle in Joe's hands. Quickly he placed it on the floor and stepped away.

"It's Kara and Joe," Nate said. "The ones who… The ones I…" He looked at Kara with pleading eyes. "Just let the big guy go, I promise I can explain."

The tattooed Mariner lay prone, red bubbles breaking on his lips. Kara glared at him then she got to her feet, facing Nate. "Go on, then," she said. "Explain to me why you're trying to free John Cortez."

"We're not freeing him," Nate insisted. "It's not like that. We're just taking him away."

"Away?" Kara asked. "Away where?"

"To the *Neptune* first," Nate said. "Then back to Frisco. He needs to answer for what he's done."

"That's why he's in here!" Kara objected. "He's going to be tried and punished."

"But he's not safe," Nate insisted. "I mean, he's not

secure. As we've literally just proved. My aunt Sedna can explain it better than I can – if you come with us to the *Neptune* she'll convince you that—"

"No!" Kara shouted. "I'm not going anywhere with you, and neither is Cortez."

"Friends, please. You mustn't fight over me."

Joe looked up, his heart thumping. The cell door was swinging open, the lock dropping in pieces to the stone floor. John Cortez had grown painfully thin since they last saw him, his ice-blue eyes sunken into his narrow, watchful face. Between his fingers were ragged flaps of skin, the remains of the webbing he'd had surgically attached to his hands.

"Don't move," the closest Mariner said, turning her pistol on Cortez. "Not one step."

"But what is all this?" he asked. "I thought you'd come to kill me, but then you started yelling at each other."

"They've come to take you home," Kara said spitefully. "To a nice little cell back in Mariner country, where you'll be warm and cosy and—"

"It's not like that," Nate snapped. "You don't know what you're talking about, Kara. We're taking him, it's been agreed."

"Agreed by who?" Kara demanded. "I didn't agree."

"You're right." Cortez smiled at her. "I'm perfectly

fine where I am."

"Shut up!" Nate and Kara snapped simultaneously, then the boy shook his head.

"Look, there's two choices," Nate said. "You can either put up a fight and lose, and watch us take him. Or you can come with us and, I promise, my aunt will tell you exactly what's going on."

"I think he's right," Joe put in, bracing himself for Kara's anger. "I mean, they've got guns and we haven't. But we should go along and find out what it's all about. Shouldn't we?"

Kara seethed silently, grinding her teeth. "Fine," she said. "But it had better be good."

2

The Prisoner

The *Neptune* was moored a mile south of the Wall, in the vast concrete wilderness they called the Badlands. The great ship lay in a shallow harbour between two fallen tower blocks, looking from a distance like just another large, steel-sided tanker. But Kara knew there was much more to it – the *Neptune* was an Ark, a floating town, home to over three thousand Mariners.

Nate and his companions had used an inflatable dinghy to transport Kara, Joe and their manacled prisoner back across the flooded city to the breach in the Wall, where more Mariners were waiting for them. They'd scaled the colossal rubble heap where the Houses of Parliament once stood, finding a small boat waiting on the far side. Now they were climbing a steel gangway to the Ark's foredeck, where a diminutive, grey-haired woman stood leaning on a driftwood walking stick.

"Hello, John," she said as Cortez was shoved up the steps towards her. "You've been busy since I saw you last."

"Councillor Sedna Weaver," Cortez said, his lip curling. "The boy says I have you to thank for breaking me out of that mudfoot sinkhole."

"Well, don't think you'll have an easier time of it with me," the old woman replied. "You're going in the brig until we reach Frisco, then I've asked the warden of Alcatraz to pick out a particularly damp and gloomy cell for you."

Cortez sighed, shaking his head. "We were on the same side once, you and I. What happened?"

She laughed coldly. "You became a mass murderer. Take him away."

The tattooed Mariner seized Cortez by the collar, hauling him into the ship. Kara watched him go, wondering if it was for the last time.

"Aunt Sedna," Nate said, taking the old woman's arm. "Meet Kara and Joe. Guys, this is my great-aunt. She came all this way to get me."

Sedna smiled fondly, creases forming around her eyes. "I didn't come just for you, Nate. I'm here for this old Ark, too. You've both been away too long." She clapped a hand on the *Neptune*'s railing. "And of course I came for

John. He always did have a tendency to take things too far."

"You can't have him," Kara said. "He's our prisoner – he belongs to the Shanties. You've got no right."

"I gave them the right," a voice said, and Kara turned. A red-haired figure stepped from an open hatchway, crossing towards them. Ella King had been a schoolteacher, but after the battle she'd taken charge of the relief effort and saved countless lives. When she put herself forward for the post of prime minister there was never any doubt she'd win. She was one of the few people Kara trusted – or at least, she had been. "I called off the guards. I let the Mariners take Cortez."

"But why?" Kara spluttered. "He needs to be punished. I thought that's what you wanted."

"He will be," Miss Ella said. "Councillor Sedna has assured me of that. But she also told me why we can't possibly keep him here. Cortez's old network is still active. If they made a concerted effort to free him, we wouldn't have the resources to stop them."

"John Cortez has questions to answer," Sedna told them, gesturing between the buildings to the breach in the Wall. "The attack on your Shanties didn't happen by accident, Kara. It was years in the planning. Cortez had help. He had funding. Someone stole that submarine from our dockyards and gave it to him. If I can find out who, I can bring them to justice.

"There is a rift growing between my people," she went on, her face darkening. "The Mariners have always been divided; between the isolationists who believe that our own needs must always come first, and those like myself who feel that we're part of this world and we ought to be working for the benefit of everyone in it. But Cortez and his followers are more extreme than either. They believe the Mariner way is the only way, that we should force it on others whether they want it or not. Our only chance to root out this poison is to put their leader on trial, to expose John Cortez's lies."

"I don't know you," Kara said. "How do I know you aren't secretly on his side?"

"Kara, she's my aunt," Nate said, offended. "You trust me, don't you?"

"I did, until you broke a terrorist out of jail."

Nate reddened, and Kara sighed apologetically. "Of course I trust you," she assured him. "And I want to trust your aunt too. But how do you know Cortez will be safer with you? How do you know there aren't some of his people on this ship right now, waiting for their chance to free him?"

"Um, we could go too," said a small voice, and everyone

looked down. Joe blushed as his eyes met Kara's. "That way you could keep an eye on Cortez all the time. Make sure he stays locked up."

Kara felt her heart thump. For a moment she was lost for words.

"It'd be fine with me," Sedna told them. "It might even be a good thing. Kara could appear before the Council, make another one of her speeches. Put a human face to the suffering Cortez caused, maybe even convince them to send more aid to the Shanties."

"But this is my home," Kara said, looking desperately at Miss Ella. "I'm needed here. Aren't I?"

The teacher pursed her lips. "Don't take this the wrong way, Kara, but not really. You've done your bit for the Shanties. And you know, there's going to be a giant uproar when I tell our people I let the Mariners take Cortez away. If I could tell them I sent you along to watch over him…"

Joe reached for Kara's hand. "It could be good for you, too. For us, I mean," he added quickly. "So many bad things happened here, it could help us forget about them. You did say we'd leave when the time was right. Maybe it's right now."

Kara felt her stomach churn, acid burning in the back of her mouth. She knew what Joe was getting at – she hadn't been herself lately. She'd been angry, bitter, frustrated. Was he right, could leaving the Shanties really be the answer?

She thought about what Sedna had said, that she could get more aid for her people. They desperately needed it – trade had dropped off almost completely since the City flooded, and starvation rates were rising. And if she could keep track of Cortez, too…

"I don't think I have a choice," she said, and Joe breathed a sigh of relief.

Miss Ella smiled, and Sedna nodded thoughtfully. Nate's grin was so wide his jaw was practically unhinged. "It's going to be so amazing," he said. "I can show you all the best places – we'll have so much fun you won't ever want to go home."

He spread his arms like he was going to hug her, but Kara backed away. "This isn't about having fun," she said sharply. "I'm going for the Shanties, and for Cortez. Not for a holiday."

And she turned and marched away across the deck.

Kara stood at a high railing as the *Neptune* moved off, feeling the Ark's massive turbines rumbling beneath her. Miss Ella had departed some time before, climbing into a small dinghy and heading back towards the harbour. The Shanties were a shrinking haze on the dark water, and she wondered how long it would be before she saw her home again.

She shouldn't have snapped at Nate, she knew that. He cared about her – a little too much, perhaps, but there was nothing she could do about that. She wondered if there'd ever come a time when she was free to just live her own life and not worry about what anyone else wanted. Even Joe felt like a burden sometimes, however much she loved him.

She looked down at her split knuckles, remembering how she'd launched herself at the tall Mariner, ignoring his size and his strength as fury overwhelmed her. It was a scary feeling, but not an unfamiliar one. It was as though there was an angry force inside her, just below the surface, ready to rise up and overwhelm her if she let it. She wondered if this was how it started for Cortez, that he got so bitter at the world that he just stopped caring about the consequences of his actions.

But would going to Frisco make that feeling better, or worse? Perhaps Joe was right, perhaps staying in the Shanties was making them both miserable. Everywhere she went there were ghosts of the past, echoes of the choices she'd made. She'd almost let Cortez burn to death that night on the submarine, and the memory of it haunted her. And sometimes she wished she had, and that haunted her even more.

"They said you were on board," a voice echoed suddenly from the dark. "I didn't believe it."

Kara turned to see a girl in a blue uniform approaching across the deck, her hands clasped in front of her. To her surprise, she found herself smiling. Cane had been her enemy once, but in the end Cortez's daughter had stepped up and done the right thing. They'd both been through so much; if anyone understood how Kara was feeling, perhaps it was her.

"I didn't know you were still here," Kara said. "In the Shanties, I mean. I assumed you'd left when they took away the rest of your father's people."

Cane blushed. "They asked, but I didn't want to go. I've been helping out in a school near Stratford Ponds. Miss Ella set it up and I ... I asked her not to tell you. I just wanted to be left alone."

Kara turned this over in her mind. Maybe it made sense, after everything that had happened. "But now you're going home."

"I didn't have a choice. Councillor Sedna wants me to give evidence to her committee."

Kara laughed. "You sound thrilled."

"I don't really know what to expect," Cane admitted. "My grandmother, my cousins, they were big supporters of my father. I'm worried how they'll react when they see me. The family traitor."

"But you're not a traitor," Kara insisted. "You stopped things from getting a lot worse."

"That won't be how they see it. I turned against him, that's all they know."

"So you'll set them straight," Kara said. "You'll tell them what really happened. Come on, you know what's right and what's wrong. Maybe they'll try to tell you otherwise but you're tough, you can handle it."

Cane blushed. "Th-thanks," she said. "From you, that means a lot."

They were clear of the buildings now, and looking over the railing Kara saw a pair of huge hatches sliding open in the side of the ship. From these openings the Disc unfolded, rubbery blue material rolling out like the world's biggest carpet. Mariners strode out, attaching the edges of the Disc to a ring of steel cables that swung down from overhead. The mighty raft snapped taut, riding the waves as the *Neptune* plied its way into the Atlantic.

Kara sighed. "You know, I swore to myself I'd stay away from Mariners from now on. I just wanted to live a quiet life, keep my head down and be a normal person."

Cane laughed out loud. "I'm sorry. But Kara, you couldn't be a normal person if you tried."

3
Pirates

They settled into life aboard the *Neptune*, their days dictated by the rising of the sun, the rhythm of the tides and the rota of work duties that Councillor Sedna insisted they all sign up to. Joe found himself gutting fish and sieving buckets of algae, scrubbing the decks with an iron brush and washing Mariner uniforms in giant mechanical tubs. He'd dropped hints about being assigned to the arboretum or the research labs, but according to Nate you needed to have something called qualifications, and he didn't.

The three of them were housed in a two-room pod, one of the tent-like domes down on the Disc where the Mariners lived while they were at sea. Joe and Kara were again sharing a bed, which was still not very restful – he wondered what could be on her mind, keeping her awake till all hours. Cortez was locked securely in the brig, three floors down on the central ship they called the Hub – she checked several times a day to make sure. The Shanties were far behind, and Miss Ella was looking after things back there anyway. So why was Kara still so distracted?

And she wasn't the only one. Nate seemed on edge too, always asking Kara if she was OK and making sure she had everything she needed. He was eager and excitable one minute, sullen and sorry-looking the next. Joe thought he knew why, but he tried not to think about it.

Their course was set for the Shoals of Panama, the swampy channel between the continents of North and South America. Once through, they'd turn north for California, following the coast until they reached Frisco. Joe couldn't wait – hour by hour the anticipation built until he found himself scrubbing the deck with frantic intensity, urging the Ark to pick up speed, wishing away the days and weeks until they reached their destination.

One night he awoke in darkness, hearing shouts outside the pod. There'd been warnings of a storm the evening before but it was too far off for the *Neptune*'s weather computer to accurately gauge its strength. Now Joe could hear powerful winds howling around the Hub, and feel the Disc shuddering as waves lashed hard against it. Kara was already out of bed, standing in the curtained doorway and peering out into the dark.

"I think it's bad," she said. "I heard someone shouting, then a medic ran past."

"What do we do?" Joe asked, gripping the wall of the dome. "Go out and see what's—"

A horn sounded, two short blasts then a longer one. Nate sat up, looking around blearily. "That's the evacuation signal. Get your stuff, they're going to fold the Disc."

Joe snatched up the pack containing his scorched plastic bear, Growly, along with a book on Mariner history that Sedna had given him. Then he followed Nate out into the darkness, the shouts of sailors echoing through the driving rain. They could see the hatch in the side of the Hub standing open, electric light blazing from the hangar within. People hurried between the domes, bundling their possessions and making for the narrow bridge that led into the ship.

Joe heard cables grind and turning back he saw the edge of the Disc rolling up behind them, the material folding back on itself as tall waves crashed over it. Beyond the Ark he could see the storm front approaching, a boiling black barrier lit by flashes of intermittent lightning.

He took Kara's hand, steadying himself as they stepped into the steel hangar. The wind screamed through the open sides as a Mariner took their names and checked them against a list on his computer tablet. Cane hurried towards them, reaching out to squeeze Joe's shoulder.

"There's nothing to be scared of. Nate and me have done this plenty of times, haven't we?"

"Actually, no," Nate admitted. "I'd only been on board a couple of weeks when everything went bad before. This is my first storm at sea."

"Well, you've trained for it," Cane reassured him. "Just remember what they taught you back at— Hey, what's going on?"

An internal door had swung open and uniformed Mariners began swarming into the hangar. They carried heavy assault weapons, forming a defensive line by the open hatchway and aiming out into the dark. "What's happening?" Cane asked one of them. "Are we under attack?"

"Ships approaching," a young woman told her. "Three vessels on an intercept course. And they're not ours."

With a clunk the winches stopped, the Disc still only half-folded. Joe clung to Kara as they gazed out into the roiling darkness. Waves crashed against the ship, water sluicing into the open hangar.

Then he saw a light in the distance, sweeping over the churning sea. He couldn't gauge the size of the ship, just a dark shape riding the waves.

"Pirates," Cane said. "It must be."

"But that's crazy," Nate objected. "Why would they attack a ship this size, in a storm? It doesn't make any s—"

Something slammed into the Ark, exploding with orange fire. The Hub lurched violently, tipping backward then splashing down. The ocean flooded in, sluicing around their ankles.

"That was a rocket blast," Cane said in disbelief. "Get down, here comes another!"

This time the impact was right above their heads, and Joe saw fragments of twisted metal hissing into the water. He heard a rising rumble and through the rain he could see a small craft drawing closer, an inflatable pilot ship crammed with figures in black wetsuits. They raised rifles and began to fire, aiming wildly as the waves pitched beneath them.

Bullets clanged off the roof and walls of the hangar, spraying sparks. The lights in the ceiling shattered, plunging them into darkness. There was a chorus of screams.

Then the Mariners returned fire, the flare from their gun barrels lighting up the night. Nate had disappeared and Joe looked around for him, his heart hammering.

41

Then he was back, thrusting an object into Joe's hand, something bulky and soft.

"It's a life jacket," Nate said. "Strap it on. Kara, you t—"

There was a flash of white light and the hangar tipped again. Joe felt a wave of heat as the rocket burst, throwing him off his feet. He splashed to the hard steel floor, slipping as he tried to stand.

Then the ship righted itself and a wave crashed through the opening, rolling over him. He was swept away as the water retreated; he heard Kara cry out but he couldn't see her. He was on his back and there was salt in his eyes – everything was dark and blurry.

He gripped the life jacket, the water turning him over and over, gunfire bellowing around him. He slid from the hangar and kept slipping, the ocean dragging him back across the half-folded Disc. His backpack was jerked from his hand and he twisted, trying to grab it without letting go of the life jacket. But the current was too forceful; his pack was lost, tumbling out to sea. And Joe was tumbling too, sucking in water, coughing helplessly, reaching out for something, anything to hold on to.

Amazingly, he found it.

It was a hand, clammy and shaking as it locked around Joe's wrist. For a moment his eyes cleared and he saw Nate staring back, his face white with terror. The wind wailed around them, the world lurching and twisting and trying to drag them apart. They hit a soft barrier, washing up against the lip of the Disc. But the waves were too strong, dragging them up and over and out into open water.

Joe managed to right himself, wiping his eyes frantically. He could see the side of the Hub, light blazing out. Shots flew in both directions, the black-clad pirates trying to force their way on board, the Mariner soldiers determined to drive them back. He saw Cane in a knot of troops, a pistol in her hand, blasting and yelling.

Then for the briefest moment he saw Kara on the edge of the hangar, gripping the frame and looking out to sea. She slipped the life jacket over her head, strapping it tight. Joe shouted but a wave washed over him and he was driven back, clinging to Nate as the sea took them. Kara stepped to the edge of the hangar, scanning the black water. For an instant their eyes locked.

Another wave crashed, driving Joe down into the dark. He gripped Nate's hand as they surfaced. The Ark was further away now, and dwindling. But there was a shape low in the water, outlined by a fork of lightning, splashing furiously. Joe shouted and Kara saw him, lowering her head and kicking, taking his arm as another wave rolled in, driving them further from the safety of the Ark.

"You … shouldn't have … jumped," he managed. "Now we're … all in … trouble."

"Again," Kara managed, before the water dragged them back under.

4

The Magic Kingdom

The sun rose over an empty ocean. The storm had passed and there was no sign of the Ark or the pirate ships, or anything but still blue water. Beneath them all was shadow and Kara could only imagine how deep it went, down and down into the endless, trackless…

"Don't think about it," Joe said. "It doesn't help."

She focused on his face peering above the inflated collar of his life jacket. The vest was made from RPV, a Mariner material that could alter its shape and texture on command. In the dark of night, as they clung together in the storm, Nate had shown them how to activate it, puffing it up so it fit snugly around their bodies. Now he bobbed nearby, snoring softly, tied to Kara and Joe by lengths of strong cord. The three of them drifted in slow circles, but everywhere she looked the view was the same.

"I knew we shouldn't have left the Shanties," she said bitterly. "I told you, didn't I?"

"I lost my bear," Joe said. "But, hey, at least we didn't drown. Or get shot by pirates."

Kara sighed. "Honestly, why are you always so cheerful? We're lost at sea, we're probably going to die of starvation, and you're all la-di-da, at least the sun's out."

Joe flushed. "I just try and see the good side, that's all. And you don't know we're going to die – we might get rescued or washed to shore."

"What shore?" Kara demanded. "Even if we did find land, we're two thousand miles from home and even further from Frisco. And America's a total war zone, even I know that."

Her voice had grown louder and Nate groaned, waving a hand. "Just gimme five more..." Then realisation crashed in and he jerked upright. "Kara, what...? Where...?"

"The Ark's gone," she told him as he scanned the horizon desperately. "They left us."

"That's impossible," Nate protested, craning to inspect a small blinking light on his left shoulder. "I activated the tracker. They should've picked us up by now."

"Maybe they had other things to worry about," Joe said. "Maybe those pirates took over the ship."

Nate took a ragged breath, trying to calm himself. "It's OK," he said. "These jackets are made for this – at the Academy they said you could survive for weeks in one if you had to." He reached down, unclipping a small zippered sack. "Look, we've got protein tablets, and this bottle has a built-in saline filter so we can drink the seawater. And over here's a flashlight, and a knife in case anything comes along that we want to eat."

"Or that wants to eat us," Kara said, inspecting the serrated blade attached to her jacket.

"There's a compass in the hilt, too," Nate pointed out. "And we can't be too far from land, pirates never attack in mid-ocean. It's weird they were there at all, actually – they don't normally go for the full-size Arks. Anyway, I think our best bet is to head west, try to hit Florida or somewhere."

"But it could still be miles, couldn't it?" Kara asked. "We can't swim that far."

"We won't have to." Nate paddled closer, reaching for Kara's hand and guiding it. "There's a little switch, just under your armpit. Here."

Kara felt a small, hard button the size of her thumbnail. "Do I just—"

She pushed it and her suit jerked forward, the cords tightening, pulling Joe and Nate with her. She let go and

47

the motion stopped.

"It's a solar-powered propeller," Nate said. "Not fast, but a lot easier than swimming. I don't know how much storage the batteries have but if we only use one at a time I bet we could keep going all day and maybe even all night."

Joe beamed at Kara. "You see? We've got food and water and we even sort of know where we're going. If you think positive, good things happen."

Kara snarled at him. "I'll remind you of that when we're getting eaten by sharks."

She powered up her propeller, pulling Joe and Nate through the water like a tugboat. At midday the sun's glare was fierce, but the suits came equipped with an erectable shade and thanks to the filter bottles, their water supply was inexhaustible. By early afternoon Kara's batteries were drained and Joe took over, settling back comfortably as the water surged around his life vest. As the hours passed, Kara found herself almost relaxing, sucking on a sugar-coated protein tablet and watching the ocean roll by. By sundown Nate was out in front, inspecting his compass as they bobbed towards the firelit horizon. Kara dozed off to the drone of his propeller and the soft splash of the waves.

* * *

He woke her before dawn and she nodded drowsily, activating her motor. The moon had set but the stars were brilliant overhead, a luminous garland reflected in the flat sea. It made her feel tiny, just an insignificant dot against the vastness of the ocean, and the world, and the universe beyond. But in an odd sort of way it made her feel important too, part of something grand. She wondered where the next days and weeks would take them, and if they'd ever make it to Mariner country.

It was late on the second day when they saw the gull, just a wheeling speck against the clouds. Nate watched it keenly. "Another day or two," he said, "if we're lucky."

But in the end it didn't take that long. As the sky grew pale the next morning Kara spotted something on the horizon and quickly woke the others. It was a pale, ladder-like structure, obviously man-made, rising from the sea in a perfect arc. Nate shielded his eyes.

"I can't make it out," he said. "Maybe it was part of a building but the rest crumbled away."

"Hey, look," Joe said, squinting down into the water. "It's getting shallow."

He was right – beneath them Kara could see patches of silty sand dotted with black rock and clumps of wrack. They had to be nearing the shore.

By the time the sun was overhead the seaweed had

begun to brush against their ankles, thick clots of it covering the sea floor. Not long afterwards Kara touched ground for the first time, breathing a sigh of relief as she stood for a moment, her rubber sandals sinking in the muck. Soon they were half-wading, half-swimming through a saltwater swamp, using the life jackets to stay afloat.

The shape in the distance was clearer now – two twisted metal pipes linked by regular diagonal struts. The arc was part of a larger structure, winding back on itself like a coil of rope.

"I've heard of this," Nate said. "I think it's what they called a rollercoaster – it was something they did for fun back in the Tech Age. Like a train running on rails. But really fast and short."

"Like me," Joe pointed out.

As they slogged on, other shapes began to appear on the horizon: a giant ribbed dome patterned with moss and green algae; a beached ship with steel masts and a dark, flaking hull; the head of some huge cartoon creature with circular black ears and a salt-rotted grin. Closer to them, smaller objects rose from the swamp: boxy hulks that Joe identified as cars, all washed against each other in great rusted heaps. Sometimes they were forced to leave the water and scale these rickety barriers, scrambling across roofs and bonnets, watching for spikes of steel and shattered glass.

It was from the top of a particularly high and treacherous junk pile that Kara first spotted the settlement. A cluster of towers rose from the water, but these weren't square and blocky like the ones at home. They were slender and cylindrical, with blue roofs and rusty spires, branching from a larger structure half sunk in the water and the weeds. Encircling this central building was a network of walkways lashed to wooden pilings, rough-hewn and ramshackle but clearly still in use. There were even a few rowing boats moored to the outer jetties, bobbing on the crystal waves.

"It looks like the Shanties," Joe said. "Only smaller."

"It could be dangerous," Nate warned. "It might be a pirates' lair."

"I feel like pirates would have better boats," Kara said. "Anyway, we don't have a choice. We need to work out where we are, and it's not like the next place we come to will be any less shady."

They waded towards the encampment, letting down their life jackets so the RPV hung loose around their bodies. Reaching a jetty, they clambered up. Kara kept the cord of her knife wrapped around her hand as they moved towards the central building. The whole place was silent, just the creaking of the boards and the cry of gulls perched on the tower tops.

The peaked structure loomed over them, clearly in a state of some disrepair. The outside was supposed to look like brick but as they drew closer Kara saw that it was just a paint job, flaking away to reveal wooden clapboard underneath. In the near side was an arched doorway, and from inside they could hear the murmur of voices and the clink of glassware.

"That sounds fun," Joe said, pointing to a plank nailed beside the doorway, where the words 'MAGIC KINGDOM' had been scrawled haphazardly in red paint.

"What's so magic about it?" Nate wondered. "I don't like this, you guys."

"Neither do I," Kara said. And she leaned on the door, inching it open with a rusty groan.

The voices stopped abruptly and twenty heads swivelled in their direction. Kara saw men and women, the former heavily bearded, the latter weathered and mean-looking. They sat around plastic tables sipping from chipped ceramic cups, and Kara could smell the tang of home-brewed Selkie.

"No, no, no!" a voice called out. "No kids allowed in the Magic Kingdom."

A ruddy-faced woman stepped from behind the makeshift bar, waving a filthy cloth.

"We just need—" Kara began but the bartender cut her off.

"Nobody cares. Whatever sob story you got about your folks being stole by pirates or et by gators, we don't want to know. Just leave before I call Big Mickey."

"But you don't understand," Nate objected. "Our ship w—"

"Mickey!" the woman screeched. "Get out here. We got trouble!"

A man shoved through a doorway, almost filling it. He wore a white apron spattered with red and in one hand he grasped a huge cleaver.

"No trouble," Nate said, retreating to the door. "We get it. We're leaving."

"Wait," Kara said, holding her ground as the man stormed towards her. "We just need some help. We have money."

The cleaver stopped in mid-swing. The bartender's eyes narrowed.

"What sort of money?" she asked. "Show us."

"We don't have it with us," Kara admitted. "But we can pay hard cash to anyone who'll help us get back to the M—"

"There you are!" a voice cried, and Kara turned in surprise. A figure stepped from the shadows at the back of the room, striding towards them. "Dang, cuz, I've been waiting for you all day."

The newcomer had dusty hair swept up in twin spikes, flashing yellow eyes ringed with black paint and a mangy fur coat mottled with threadbare patches. From the voice Kara thought it was a girl, but in the dim light she couldn't be sure. A firm hand took hold of her wrist and she started to pull away, but the stranger leaned in close.

"Kara, be cool. Just follow my lead."

The sound of her own name shocked Kara into silence. The stranger turned to smile at the crowd, exposing rows of filed teeth, pointed and capped with silver. "Now, there's no cause for alarm. This here's my second cousin twice removed – Jenny. She's been slapping oars all night from upcoast and I reckon she's got herself a mite addled from sleep deprivement. Ain't that right, Jen?"

Kara was fixed with a stern stare, and to her surprise she found herself nodding. "Um, right."

"And these here youngins –" the stranger indicated Nate and Joe – "are my other second cousin Fred and their good old pal from back home, whose name is, um, Shrimpy."

Joe opened his mouth to protest, then thought better of it.

"She said they had money," the bartender protested, gesturing at Kara. "She said there was money for someone who'd take them somewhere. Muh-something, I was listening."

"Oh, no, she said *honey*," the stranger insisted. "She could give you all the honey you want if you take her back to her, um, mother. Who is a beekeeper. In Baton Rouge."

The bartender scowled. "That sounds pretty far-fetched to me. They walked into our place. I say they're ours to deal with. Right, Mick?"

Mickey grunted and took a step forward, gripping his cleaver.

But the stranger stood firm, one hand straying towards a belted holster where a silver pistol hung. "Listen, you know who I work for and you know why I'm here. So I suggest you back off, right now, unless you want more aggravation than you can handle."

The bartender's face flushed and Kara heard the clunk as she shut her mouth.

"Now we're headed to my cutter," the stranger went on, drawing Kara to the door and kicking it open with one booted foot. "But it's been awful nice meeting you all, and I hope to be back real soon in your charming little burg. Bye now."

Kara was yanked through the door, Nate and Joe on her heels. Out in the light she saw that the stranger was barely older than she was, grinning through those weird silver fangs. "If you want to get back to the Mariners, you'll come with me. Those limpets in there might be slow, but it won't take 'em long to figure out you're no cousin of mine. My boat's this way."

The stranger marched away along the jetty but before Kara could follow, Nate grabbed her jacket. He leaned close, Joe squeezed between them.

"I don't like this," Nate hissed. "Who is that person? Where did they come from? Is it even a girl or a boy?"

"I think neither," Joe said. "Back in the Shanties we had a teacher who—"

"Is it important?" Kara cut in. "Besides, what other choice is there? Stay here?"

They turned as the door to the Magic Kingdom creaked open and Big Mickey stepped out, swinging his cleaver. Nate's eyes went wide and he gulped. "Hey, cousin!" he shouted. "Wait for us!"

They hurried after the stranger, weaving through a twisted spiderweb of jetties, shacks and unsteady walkways. Kara caught up, striding alongside.

"Back there, you knew my name. How?"

The stranger snorted. "Everyone knows your name, Kara. Everyone's seen your clip, except for inbred backwater clambuckets like that lot back there."

"What clip?" Kara asked. "What are you talking about?"

"Your speech?" the stranger said, enunciating carefully as if Kara wasn't too bright. "Persuading your people to stand up to the Mariners? Couple of months back you couldn't walk two blocks without some news jockey trying to screen it for you."

"You mean…" Joe said, his mouth hanging open. "You mean Kara's famous?"

"You could say that," the stranger said, shrugging. "I mean, I don't really see what all the fuss is about – I figure anyone could've said that stuff. But it was pretty popular. Got a lot of folks talking."

"You know not all Mariners are like Cortez, right?" Nate asked nervously. "Some of us are OK."

"Whatever. All I care about is how much they'll give me for bringing you home."

"So you're a mercenary?" Nate scowled.

"I'm whatever I'm paid to be. Smuggler, sailor, trader. Jack of all trades."

Kara smiled despite herself. "So, Jack, do you have a name?"

The stranger turned, putting out a hand. "The name's Lynx, and I am mightily pleased t—"

Shouts rose behind them and Kara twisted, shielding her eyes. Back along the jetty she saw the bartender breaking into a run, the machete-wielding cook lumbering at her side.

"Last chance," Lynx said. "Come with me, or stay with them."

"I'm in," Joe said.

"And me," Kara agreed.

Nate rolled his eyes. "Fine."

At the end of the pier was a battered trawler with a wooden cab and the name *Ursula* stencilled on the side. "You, cast off," Lynx said, gesturing at Nate. "Kara, grab the wheel. I'll start her up."

They bounded on to the deck, Lynx tugging open a metal hatch and dropping inside. Kara heard a strange groan beneath her feet but it was soon drowned out by the rattle of the engine, chemical smoke pouring from an exhaust pipe at the back. Through the glass of the cab she could see the bartender waving her arms, then Lynx reappeared, slamming the hatch down.

"Well, what are we waiting for?"

Kara shoved the stick forward, feeling the boat move away from the jetty. Joe and Nate stood in the stern, watching as the bartender skidded to the edge of the pier, her furious cries barely audible over the din of the motor.

"You get back here, you little punk!" she bellowed. "You didn't pay for your drinks!"

5

The Gulf

They spent the night on the *Ursula*'s deck, surrounded by ropes and tackle and mysterious wooden crates, the stink of chem fuel filling Joe's nostrils as he curled against Kara's side. Lynx held the wheel with one hand, humming an ancient song about a ring of fire while the stars turned overhead. Joe wasn't sure why, but he liked the young smuggler. Lynx had a funny way of talking that he didn't quite understand, but they seemed genuinely eager to help. Maybe it was only for the money, but that seemed pretty normal in this world. He doubted if Kara would've done any different.

As the sun rose he sat up and took his bearings. The water around them was dark and polluted, glittering with patches of oil. In the distance he saw a steel structure floating on the ocean, rocking from side to side with a dull, ominous clang.

"Where are we?" he asked and Lynx turned, fixing on a smile that didn't look quite true.

"This is the Gulf of Mexico. I know these waters well. I'll get you where you need to go."

"Why have we turned west?" Nate asked, sitting up beside Joe and checking the compass on his life jacket. "From where we started I thought the Shoals of Panama would be south, or south west at least."

"This is the best heading," Lynx assured him. "Go dead south and you wind up in the Caribbean, where there's more pirates than palm trees. But, hey, if you *want* to be a galley slave…"

"It's fine," Kara said, rubbing her eyes. "You pick the heading."

Nate frowned, whispering behind his hand. "I don't like this."

"So you keep saying," Kara hissed back. "But we're here now, aren't we? And I don't think Lynx is planning to hurt us, I just don't get that feeling."

Nate flushed. "What feeling do you get? I just think we should— Hey, is that land?"

Joe shielded his eyes as the sky grew lighter. There was a dark haze on the horizon and he heard the cry of gulls.

"You said we were making for Panama," Nate protested.

61

"Not across the Gulf."

Lynx shrugged, trying to seem casual. "We need fuel. We won't make it on two tanks."

"So why didn't you say anything before?" Kara asked, getting to her feet.

"It's clear you don't trust me. I didn't want to alarm you for no good reason."

"I trust people who give me the facts," Kara said, pushing past Lynx and cutting the engine. "Now we're not going anywhere until you tell us what's going on."

Lynx hesitated and in the silence Joe heard a noise – a kind of muffled groan. He'd heard it when they first came on board but now it was louder, more insistent. It seemed to be coming from under his feet.

"I'm telling you, it's no big deal," Lynx was saying. "We'll fuel up, then we'll be on our way."

"That's a lie," Nate spluttered. "This has to be a set-up."

Joe got down on his knees, peering through a gap in the deck. He squinted, sure he could see something moving. Then an eye blinked open and he cried out, leaping to his feet.

"There's someone down there!" he shouted. "Someone underneath us!"

Lynx tried to shove forward but Nate got there first, reaching for the hatch and pulling it open. His face fell.

On the floor of the ship's hold lay a dark-haired woman, bound at the wrists and ankles with a gag stuffed in her mouth. She was wide awake, staring up at them with pleading eyes.

"I gave her a sleeping shot before I tied her up," Lynx said, annoyed. "Seems it's worn off."

Kara took hold of Lynx's lapels, shoving the smuggler back against the boat's railing.

"What is she doing down there?"

Lynx wrenched a hand free, pushing Kara away. The two of them stood nose to nose.

"She stole from the wrong people," Lynx said. "I was sent to fetch her back."

"So you're a bounty hunter too?" Kara spat. "You really are a jack of all trades."

"Hey, it wasn't easy," Lynx protested. "I've been tracking her for weeks. I thought the trail had gone cold a couple times, but you'd be amazed what secrets people part with if you mention you work for The Five."

"What's The Five?" Joe asked, but Lynx ignored him.

Nate tightened the straps on his life jacket, peering down into the murky water. "I'd rather take my chances back in the ocean than rely on this … outlaw one second longer."

"Don't be crazy," Lynx said. "You can't just jump overboard."

"Why not?" Kara asked, glancing at the pistol on Lynx's belt. "Would you shoot us?"

"Probably not," Lynx admitted. "But you won't get far. Look."

Joe heard a high-pitched drone, coming closer. Scanning the ocean he spotted a black speck, then another. A pair of jetskis, riding low and fast through the oily sea.

"It's like I said," Lynx told Kara. "You're famous. People will want to meet you. But you won't be hurt, I swear. Not unless you make trouble."

"Shut up now," Kara said, and turned her back.

The jetskis circled the *Ursula*, engines clattering. Joe studied their passengers – a boy and a girl, both close to Kara's age. The girl had a pierced lip and orange stripes in her hair, bright against her dark-brown scalp. The boy had a tangle of curls like a mane down his back and his gloves were capped with silver claws, gripping the handlebars of his ski.

They cut their engines and the striped girl raised a hand. "Morning, Lynx. We were starting to wonder when you'd be back."

"Who are your new friends?" the boy asked. "Ain't you going to introduce us?"

Lynx gestured at Kara. "Use your eyes. It's the girl from the clip, the one The Five couldn't get

64

enough of, remember?"

The girl gave a whistle. "That's some catch."

Lynx grinned. "I know, right? Now, Kara, these here are the Wildcats, my very own pack. Golden-locks over there is Leo, and this cute little kitten calls herself Tigress."

That was it, Joe realised. Each of the three had styled themselves after a different big cat – lion, tiger and lynx. Their clothes, their hair, their tattoos, even the jewellery they wore – it all added to the effect.

The lion boy drifted closer, scanning the boat. "So where's the traitor?"

Lynx pointed down. "Safe and secure."

"You meet any trouble?" the tiger girl asked.

Lynx shrugged. "None I couldn't handle. Now come on, we've got ground to cover if we still want to make the big bash."

Lynx steered for shore, the horizon coalescing into a skyline pricked with crumbling tower blocks. The city had been grand once, Joe could tell, but decades of erosion had taken their toll. It was even more derelict than London now, few blocks standing more than a few storeys, with heaps of oil-streaked rubble sloping between them.

They turned north, into a channel between banks of submerged concrete. On the shoreline Joe could see a peculiar white shape – a vehicle of some sort, but not one he'd ever seen before. It resembled the airplanes in Miss Ella's clips, only chunkier and wider, with a black nose and letters painted on the tail – an 'N' and an 'A'. Then he realised.

"That's a spaceship!"

Lynx grinned. "Space *shuttle*, if you know your history. This is Houston – it's where they sent rockets up, back in the real olden days."

"Do they still?" Joe asked excitedly. "Do any of them still fly?"

Lynx laughed. "If there was a way off this planet, I know a few folk who'd have took it by now."

Beyond the city the towers thinned, replaced by rows of giant steel tanks linked with pipes and girders. Dark figures swarmed between them, wearing padded suits and oil-smeared helmets. There was a whoosh and a pillar of flame erupted from one of the pipes; even from this distance Joe could feel the heat on his face.

"What is this place?" he asked.

"Oil refinery," Lynx said. "Wildcat operation. Literally."

"But the Gulf rigs were shut down centuries ago," Nate objected. "We learned about it in history class – they sucked up every last drop."

"There's still oil down there, if you know which bits of

the sea floor to rip up. And it just so happens The Five do."

Nate frowned. "That's horrible. The Gulf has a unique ecosystem."

Lynx laughed. "Spot the Mariner."

"That's the third time you've mentioned this Five," Kara said. "Who are they – some kind of gang?"

Lynx cut the engine and they drifted, bumping up against the concrete sea wall. "Round these parts The Five are everything. Moon, sun, and stars in the sky. Some folks would give their right arm to meet them in person. Hopefully you won't have to."

After weeks at sea it was strange being back on solid ground – Joe's stomach kept rolling queasily, and the stench of petroleum didn't help. The other Wildcats had parked their jetskis and now Leo ambled over, inspecting Nate and his deflated life jacket.

"This is Mariner merchandise," he said. "Is that what you are, boy?"

Nate flushed. "Yes, actually. So don't mess with me or you'll have an Ark to deal with."

Leo took hold of the jacket, snapping the straps and tugging it free, almost dragging Nate off his feet. "Hey!" he protested. "That's mine."

Leo grinned. "Not any more."

Lynx waved a hand. "Leave him be, he's harmless."

Leo drew the serrated knife from its holster, holding it up. "You think?"

He crossed to Kara and Joe, gesturing for their jackets and slinging them over his arm. Then Lynx ushered them forward, across the dock towards a pair of huge eight-wheeled vehicles with oval-shaped tanks on the back. Refinery workers bustled around with lengths of rubber hose and the concrete was black with spilled oil.

Tigress joined them, leading the prisoner from the *Ursula*. Behind the trucks was a smaller vehicle, a squat, rust-pocked bus painted yellow, with the letters CHO stencilled on the side.

"This is us," Lynx said, pulling a lever to make the bus doors creak open. "After you, please."

Kara paused, fixing the smuggler with a hard stare. "I don't know where you're taking us," she said, "or what you and this ... Five have got planned. But I warn you, if Joe gets hurt, or Nate, I'm going to hold you personally responsible."

Lynx blanched for a moment, then forced a silver-pointed smile. "I told you, there's nothing to worry about. We're going to a big gathering in the desert. They'll be coming in from all over to join the crusade. Trust me, it's going be fun."

6

The Show

The yellow bus was ancient and rusted, with holes in the corrugated floor so they could see the cracked tarmac passing underneath. Kara gripped the metal bench, the walls rattling around her, the din of the engine loud in her ears. It just isn't natural, she thought. People weren't meant to travel so fast, except maybe in a boat where the going was smoother and it didn't feel like your innards were going to leap through your mouth every time you hit a pothole.

Lynx was driving, hunched over the large black steering wheel. There was no glass in the windscreen, just a pair of metal plates with a gap in the middle to see through. Up ahead were the oval-shaped tanker trucks, sending up clouds of dust as they rumbled over the dry desert road. And darting between them were two swift cars piloted by the other Wildcats, each one body-painted to match its owner, with eyes on the headlamps and snarling mouths on the engine grilles. Lynx's own dun-coloured vehicle was chained to the back of the bus, dragging along behind.

"Hey, there are people out there," Joe said in surprise, squinting through the window. This was shielded too, but the steel was pocked with small holes that must have been made by bullets.

"How do they survive?" Nate asked, leaning over Joe to peer out. "Everything's so … dead."

He was right – through a crack in her own window Kara could see the wasteland that surrounded them, dotted with the carcasses of houses, vehicles and barns. Packs of dogs roamed the hills and occasionally there were dark figures at the roadside, clad from head to toe in filthy rags. They kept their distance as the convoy rattled through, taking shelter in gullies and culverts.

"They call this the DustRoad," Lynx said. "Runs all the way from sea to shining sea. Farther inland is outlaw country, nothing but bandits and cannibal cults, and thieving scum like that one back there." The prisoner had been shackled to the rearmost bench, staring forward in sullen silence. "But this is The Five's territory and, believe it or not, they are making improvements. For years this whole state has been deader than a Mariner at a pirate party. Nothing living, nothing growing. But that's starting to change. Look."

The smuggler gestured down into a stony valley, the road hugging the higher slopes. At the bottom Kara could see a slender ribbon of reflected light: a stream, barely a trickle. But to either side the land was transformed – green stems waved in the breeze, irrigation pumps spraying clear water. There were solar panels on the concrete roofs and workers in the fields, wide-brimmed hats shielding their faces. Crows circled and goats lounged in patches of shade.

"There are ranches like this all over now," Lynx explained. "The Five raised me up from nothing. They gave me a direction, a purpose. Now they're doing the same for this whole deadbeat country."

"So those are The Five's slaves?" Nate asked.

Lynx snorted. "We're not savages, kid. They're workers – they get fed, they get meds, they can leave any time if they got somewheres else to go, though not many do. And best of all they get the chance to serve The Five directly, to be recruits for the cause."

"What cause?" Kara asked. "What are The Five really up to?

Lynx smiled enigmatically. "Oh, you'll find out. Real soon."

By late afternoon, Kara was beginning to understand. They were no longer the only ones on the DustRoad – a line of trucks, cars and buses stretched ahead and behind, all moving in the same direction. They came in all shapes and sizes and many were clearly handcrafted, patched and soldered from the wreckage of other vehicles, decorated with ornaments and symbols and spikes like weird metallic crustaceans. Most had weapons mounted to the hood or the roof; machine guns and rocket launchers housed in purpose-built turrets. Often a faster vehicle would pass on one side or the other, a shiny speedster or an off-road buggy, the driver tipping Lynx a nod as they rattled past. They were men for the most part, with ruddy faces, shaved heads and uniforms of brown and grey.

"What do the flags mean?" Joe asked. Almost every vehicle had a banner waving from the roof or painted on the hood; Kara saw blue crosses and red stripes, silver stars and black eagles.

"They're state flags," Lynx explained. "That one's from Kentucky, and that's from Tennessee. Some are from even further – the green banner's from Washington and the tree is Vermont."

"But aren't the states at war?" Joe asked. "That's what my teacher told me."

"Of course they are," Nate put in. "America's been

a battleground for more than a century, all except the Mariner lands in California."

"You're behind the times," Lynx said, shifting gears. "They might be flying their state flags, but look there, and there. It's not the only symbol they're showing."

It was true – on dusty hoods and rusted bumpers Kara saw another sign, a golden hand with five outstretched fingers. Some had slogans stencilled above or below – UNITE THE STATES was a popular one; AMERICA: ONE NATION another. She watched them rattle by, a sense of deep unease growing inside her.

At last the convoy slowed, tracking the curve of a muddy river fringed with weeping willows. On the far side, a city rose from the plain, cracked glass towers fracturing the purple sunset. They passed a battered sign that read EAST AUSTIN SHOWGROUNDS, entering a concrete lot filled with vehicles parked in rusted rows as far as Kara could see. Their drivers stepped out, rifles and machetes slung across their backs, pistols and water canisters strapped to their belts. They shook hands and clasped shoulders, smiling with tense anticipation.

The tankers rumbled on but Lynx found a berth, pulling the bus in and switching off the engine. "End of the line, folks."

The smuggler stood, striding to the back of the bus and yanking the prisoner to her feet. Lynx marched her back down the aisle, and as they passed Kara thought she saw something in the prisoner's hand, metal gleaming, just for a moment.

"You three as well," Lynx ordered. "And don't think about trying to run – these are all The Five's followers. You wouldn't get five yards."

Lynx led them between the tightly packed vehicles, down a gravel slope towards the tree-lined creek. There were lights up ahead now, search beams weaving in the darkling air, and the hum of voices was low and expectant. Kara remembered the time an African circus had come to the Shanties, sailing through the Cut in a painted boat laden with tents and elephants and mystics. She and Joe couldn't afford to see the show but they'd wandered through the Pavilion all night just soaking up the carnival atmosphere, the sense that anything could happen and probably would. This was the same, but with a hint of aggression just below the surface.

They passed a last line of vehicles and found themselves in a dusty field bustling with people. On a metal grille over a firepit, a man in a hat with HAIL TO THE CHEF printed on it was turning haunches of roasted dog. Kara's stomach growled and she realised she'd had nothing but protein tablets for the past four days. Still, this might not be the time to bring it up.

At the far end of the field Kara could see a truck the size of a house, a massive twenty-four-wheeler with an old advertising board on the side depicting a clown holding a meaty sandwich. The searchlights were rigged to the roof, painting the clouds in shafts and circles of white.

"It's about to start," Lynx said. "Listen."

Beneath the chatter was a new sound, a persistent drone rising in volume until Kara felt her ears tingle. Voices trailed off, expectant faces lit by the swooping lights. The sound built and built, a steady electronic pulse cutting through the still air. The anticipation became unbearable.

Then with a clunk and a crash the side of the huge truck dropped open, heavy chains slamming taut. A stage was formed, lights blazing from within, forcing Kara to shield her eyes. The drone reached a crescendo then a pounding beat kicked in, thumping so hard that dust rose from the ground. Steam hissed from silver pipes, shapes moved in the gloom and the crowd shrieked with excitement.

Five figures stepped forward, silhouetted in white. They stood with their legs together and their arms outstretched, like a row of crucifixes. Joe reached for Kara and she squeezed his fingers, her heart hammering in time with the music. Then a voice spoke, so loud that she almost bit her tongue.

"America," it said as a spotlight engulfed the central figure, throwing him into sharp relief.

"Are," said the next man, as light surrounded him too.

"You," intoned the third, the word landing like a stone.

"Ready," said the fourth, as light blazed.

"To RISE?" cried the last man, and the crowd went berserk, throwing their arms in the air and screaming. Kara saw a woman climbing on her boyfriend's shoulders, pulling off her shirt and waving it in the air. A soldier fell to his knees, clasping his hands together and weeping.

"Are you ready to rise?" the first man repeated as the audience bellowed their approval.

"Are you ready to win?" the next added, flashing white teeth.

"Are you ready to take back everything that was taken from you?" the third asked.

"We're ready," said the fourth.

"We were *born* ready," said the fifth.

Cool blue lights rose from the front of the stage and now Kara could see the men's faces, their immaculately trimmed hair and perfect smiles. But what she saw made no sense. The Five weren't just dressed the same, they were identical in every respect: the same gleaming green eyes and burnished skin, the same alert, active features. Even their movements were in flawless lockstep as they moved to the edge of the stage, striding with absolute confidence.

"It's time for every American to come together," they said, their voices overlapping.

"We've torn each other down for far too long."

"Every state at war with its neighbours."

"Every man at war with himself."

"A pattern of self-destruction that has ripped this great country to pieces."

"We need to rediscover the strength our forefathers had."

"The men who conquered the plains."

"Who drilled the oil."

"Who fought the wars and conquered the world."

One came forward, holding up his hands. "Now, we know what you're thinking."

"The past is gone."

"The world is different now."

"Different rules apply."

"And that's true." On the last word all five spoke, adding weight and emphasis.

"Things can never go back to the way they were."

"But they don't have to."

"We can make a better world."

"All of us."

"Together."

Joe's hand clenched and Kara felt her blood freeze. She knew those words. They were hers. The Five had taken lines from her speech.

"There's only one thing standing in our way," they went on as the lights dimmed and that brooding electronic tone sounded again.

"One black spot on our bright horizon."

"A group of outsiders living right on our doorstep."

"They could've helped us, but they chose not to."

"They could've shared their technology."

"Offered a guiding light as we struggled in the dark."

"But they didn't."

"They just sealed their borders."

"As the world fell into chaos."

Kara was reminded of Cortez, of the words he'd used to accuse the people of London, safe behind their wall. Then she realised who The Five were talking about and her stomach rolled over.

"The Mariners don't respect anything," they said, facing the crowd with grim faces.

"They sail round this world like they own it."

"They launch attacks against helpless cities, killing thousands."

"Threatening innocent children."

"And if they get wind of what's happening here, if they find out that a new power is rising to challenge their dominance, they'll cut us down, make no mistake."

They leaned together, their voices hushed. The field was absolutely silent, absolutely still.

"We're left with one option."

"One chance for survival."

"We have to take the fight to them."

"We have to strike first, and we have to strike hard."

"Before they know we're coming, our army will be at their gates."

"Ready to seize their technology and use it to benefit everyone."

"We'll smash their city to smithereens."

"And with the pieces we will build a new nation, proud and strong!"

They raised their heads, jaws thrust forward, teeth glistening in the swooping light. The crowd waved and hollered, punching the air, a great churning mass of wild enthusiasm. And Kara stood in silence, half horrified and half thrilled to the core, unable to fully comprehend what she'd just heard.

7

The Hunt

Lynx yanked on the chain, pulling the prisoner towards the edge of the field. Kara and Nate followed and Joe hurried along behind, his thoughts tumbling.

"I can't believe they used bits from your speech," he told Kara. "That was so crazy."

"Lynx did say they'd seen the clip," she said. "I guess they must have liked it."

"But they twisted it," Nate put in bitterly. "Your speech was about peace and they turned it into a declaration of war. They're going to attack my people. They must be mad."

Looking around, Joe wondered if he might be right. Hysteria had gripped the crowd, men and women weeping and hugging each other fiercely. A soldier fired into the air, screaming, "Death to the Mariners!" and

Nate ducked behind Kara.

They reached the rear of the stage truck, black rubber tyres rising taller than Joe's head. A steel barrier blocked the way but a man with a clipboard recognised Lynx and waved them through.

Beyond the barrier was a large enclosure ringed with fences and wagons, all lit by flickering floodlights. The place bustled with activity, people hurrying back and forth with bottles of water and crates of electrical cables. "They're coming off stage," a man barked into a short-range radio. "Get ten beers on ice and make sure those grapes are fresh."

"There you are!" a voice called and Joe looked up. The rear of the stage truck was a tangle of wires and rigging, a chem-oil generator grinding noisily. Metal steps descended and five white-clad figures came striding down, soaked in sweat.

"So you found our little runaway."

"You always come through, Lynx."

"Totally trustworthy."

"Totally reliable."

"Whatever the mission."

"It was my pleasure," Lynx managed, blushing fiercely.

"But, hey, aren't there a couple more than we asked for?" one of the men asked. "We only—"

He saw Kara and his mouth clamped shut in surprise. The man beside him looked too, and his eyes widened.

"It can't be."

"It's impossible."

"*Kara Jordan?*"

The Five pressed in, seizing Kara's hands and shaking vigorously. Up close their similarity was even more striking – every blemish, every contour was precisely the same.

"What are you doing here?" they asked.

"Did you come looking for us?"

"Or is this just the wildest coincidence in history?"

Kara tried to explain what had happened, how they'd been on course for Frisco and ended up marooned on the Florida coast. "Your … thug kidnapped us," she said, indicating Lynx.

"I knew you'd want to see her," Lynx said.

"And you were right," one of the men grinned.

"Showing terrific initiative there, Lynx," another added.

"And besides, you're better off," the next told Kara.

"You'll have a much better time with us than with those seaweed-eaters," his companion laughed.

Kara's face darkened. "We saw your speech. You've declared war on the Mariners."

The Five nodded in agreement.

"We had to."

"They deserve it."

"Hiding back there in their flashy city."

"Hoarding all the good stuff for themselves."

"Letting folks out here starve."

"You'll lose," an angry voice said and they turned as one, heads twisting like a flock of starlings. Nate stood with his fists clenched, staring furiously at The Five. "My people have technology you couldn't even dream of. They'll blast you back into the desert."

The Five studied him. "Is he the one from the speech?"

"Your Mariner friend?"

"His name's Nate," Kara said. "And this is Joe."

"Hi."

"Hi."

"Good to meet you."

"The Mariner kid looks upset."

"Didn't he like the show?"

"It was disgusting," Nate snarled. "I think you're evil."

Each of The Five raised a single eyebrow.

"We're really not."

"Honestly."

"We're just— Hey!"

Joe turned, but before he could see what was happening something slammed into his side, knocking him down in the dirt. He felt Lynx stagger on top of him, heard shouts and saw the prisoner sprinting away across the enclosure, shaking off her handcuffs as she ran.

Lynx cursed, snatching for the pistol, but one of The Five held up a hand.

"Let us handle this."

"It'll be fun."

"Like old times."

They sprang forward, heads lowered, sprinting side by side over the dusty ground. In the artificial light they looked like something from Joe's nightmares, more like a pack of wolves than a group of men. The prisoner desperately sought a way out, but she was hemmed in by trucks and steel fences. The Five broke formation, two circling outward while the other three held the centre. The prisoner saw them and picked up the pace, her eyes wide with fear.

As Joe got to his feet he saw something shiny in the dust: an inch-long spike of rusty metal that might have been prised off the bus. She must have used it to pick her handcuffs, he thought, and slipped it into his pocket.

The prisoner reached the far fence, throwing herself against it, trying to scramble up. But The Five were closing in from all sides, hollering and whooping, their white shirts glowing in the electric glare. She tried again and this time she seized the top of the fence with both hands, dragging herself up just ahead of the first two men, their hands snatching at nothing.

But one of The Five had thought ahead; he vaulted over the hood of a nearby truck, bounding on to the roof. As the prisoner swung her leg over the fence he dived from above, grabbing her around the waist and pulling her back into the enclosure. They fell together, slamming into the dirt.

Lynx hurried forward and Joe followed. The Five circled the helpless prisoner, the one who'd caught her picking himself up and mopping the dust from his brow. Just above his eye, Joe saw a small white scar. Then he stepped forward and kicked the prisoner, hard.

"You stole from us," said the scar-eyed man.

"You lied to us," his brothers agreed.

"Now you try to run away."

"Haven't you learned anything?"

"There's no running from The Five."

Scar-eye raised a booted foot, preparing to slam it down, but a voice shouted, "Wait!"

He stopped, turning. Kara had stepped in, her hands shaking. "Don't, please. You could kill her."

Scar-eye smiled coldly. "That's the idea."

"But you said you weren't evil," Kara pleaded. "Didn't you?"

The others frowned quizzically.

"Why do you care about her?"

"Are you going to make another one of your speeches?"

"Tell us how everyone has the right to life?"

"Liberty?"

"And the pursuit of happiness?"

Kara growled in frustration. "This isn't a joke, it's someone's life."

One of the men shook his head. "We're sorry, Kara."

"But this is how we do things."

"We can't let people steal from us and go unpunished."

"So punish her another way," Kara said. "She looks strong – put her on one of those ranches. Make her work for you."

The Five seemed surprised, glancing at one another.

"You know, that's not the worst idea."

"Why waste a good worker?"

"We could give her to the Austin grow-op."

Scar-eye snarled. "She made a fool of us. She deserves to die."

"I agree."

"I'm not sure."

"We should vote on it."

"All those in favour of following Kara's advice and letting her live, say aye. Aye."

"Aye.

"Aye."

Scar-eye stared at his brothers, then he sighed. "Fine. But it makes us look weak."

"Lynx, get her cleaned up and back on the bus."

"You can drop her at the ranch in the morning."

Lynx's face turned scarlet. "It took me weeks to track her down. And you're just going to let her get away with it?"

"She's not getting away," one of The Five said.

"She'll work for us."

"Pay her debt."

Lynx gestured bitterly at Kara. "And what about the girl and her friends? Should I lock them up too?"

"Oh no, they can stay with us."

"The room at the back will be just right."

"Lynx, don't pull that face."

"They're kids."

"How much trouble could they be?"

"Look at that one, he's knee high to a sandcricket."

Joe saw conflicting emotions race across Lynx's face – frustration, bitterness, even jealousy. But the young smuggler said nothing, hauling the prisoner to her feet and stalking away across the enclosure. The Five watched, shaking their heads in unison.

"You might've made an enemy there, Kara."

"Lynx has a tendency to take things sort of personally."

Then they turned as one, beckoning. "Please, step this way."

"We'll take you to our command centre."

"We think you'll like it."

At the far end of the enclosure was a large flatbed truck, and balanced on the back was the shiniest structure Joe had ever seen. It was wider than a shipping container and much longer, with square windows and wheels underneath. The exterior was corrugated steel and every inch was polished to a gleam.

"It's a train carriage," Nate realised.

"That's right," one of The Five grinned.

"An observation car," another added, pointing to a transparent dome that rose from the roof.

"All the technical stuff is on the upper deck."

"And down below are the living quarters."

"We'll get cleaned up."

"Then we can talk."

"We still can't believe it."

"Kara Jordan, right here in the flesh."

They entered the train car through a sliding door,

stepping into a long, narrow lounge with couches on both sides and a black marble bar at the far end.

"So Kara, did you notice we slipped a couple of your lines into our show?"

"If you're going to steal, steal from the best."

"It reminded me of Cortez too," she said.

"Well, we watched his speech as well."

"It was powerful stuff."

"Highly motivating."

They slipped out of their white jackets, washing their faces in a sink powered by a foot pump. Joe wondered how old they were – they looked in good shape, without an ounce of flab. But there was a tightness to their skin that seemed unnatural, a shiny, almost varnished surface.

They changed into loose-fitting black shirts stitched with the symbol of the golden hand, and as they buttoned their sleeves something caught Joe's eye. One of the men had a red birthmark on his wrist – a large spot and a short stripe, like Morse code. He noticed Joe looking and tugged his sleeve down. So they're not completely identical, Joe thought. That's interesting.

"So why were you headed to Frisco?" Scar-eye asked. "Have you joined the Mariners now?"

Kara reddened. "No, I... They told me if I went and talked to their High Council, I might be able to get some aid for my people back in the Shanties."

The Five laughed darkly.

"That sounds like the Mariners, all right."

"Making you beg for their help."

"Why do you hate us so much?" Nate asked. "What have we ever done to you?"

The Five looked at him.

"It's not so much what you've done."

"As what you haven't done."

"Not that we have to explain ourselves to you."

"Or to anyone else."

"Just trust us."

"We have our reasons."

"But let's not get into them now." The one with the birthmark was looking at Kara with concern. "They're already exhausted."

"Of course they are."

"They've come a long way."

"Forgive us."

"The guest room is this way."

They were led into a steel corridor with open doors in either wall. Inside, Joe saw five identical rooms, the beds neatly made. At the end a sixth door stood wide.

"There's only one bunk, I'm afraid."

"But it should be big enough for the three of you."

Joe yawned despite himself and Kara turned to face The Five.

"Thank you," she said. "This is … good of you."

The nearest one smiled – Joe thought it was birthmark again. "We're really not so bad."

"Once you get to know us."

"Sleep well, now."

They slid the door shut and Kara dropped on to the bed. Nate crossed to a small square window and stood there, his hands trembling.

"Those men are insane," he said. "It's the only explanation."

"They're certainly not fans of the Mariners," Kara said. "But don't worry, we'll look after you."

Nate shook his head. "I'm not worried about me. I'm worried about my people."

Kara frowned. "But don't the Mariners have all that advanced technology? Surely they'll be able to deal with a bunch of guys in trucks."

"Kara, this is an *army*," Nate said. "If they launch an attack there's no telling how much damage they'll do, how many of my people they'll kill."

"And The Five might have tech of their own," Joe pointed out. "They seem pretty confident."

"We have to stop them," Nate decided. "However we

can. Before they reach Frisco."

"But what can we do?" Kara asked. "Pop their tyres?"

"We could try sending a signal," Joe said. "Warn the Mariners so they can get ready."

"Frisco is nearly two thousand miles away," Nate said. "No radio signal could reach that far – there's too much interference. We could escape, though. Steal a car and get ahead of them, follow this DustRoad."

"You heard Lynx," Kara reminded him. "We'd be a target for bandits and slavers and even cannibals. And we'd need fuel and water and food."

"So we'll get those things," Nate snapped. "But I'm not giving up just because it's hard, Kara. I'm not scared like I used to be, and I won't let these new friends of yours attack my people. You might not care about the Mariners, but I do."

"I care," Kara said defensively. "Of course I do. But look, we only just got here. We need to find out as much as we can about The Five and their plans, not just go off half-cocked and get ourselves hurt."

Nate flushed and Joe stepped between them. "First we need to sleep," he said. "You never know, maybe in the morning things won't seem so bad."

Nate grumbled but Kara got to her feet, pulling back the covers. "Joe's right, we're exhausted. Come on, both of you. Into bed."

Nate coughed, blushing so hard that his cheeks glowed. Joe almost laughed, then caught himself.

"You know what?" he said. "I'll go in the middle."

8

The Tower of Lost Children

Soft, warm rain was falling as Cane approached the driftwood door and knocked firmly. The waterfront house was completely silent – through a glass frame she could see the entrance hall with its crossed flags and portraits of famous Mariner pioneers, and beyond that the stairs to the living quarters and the submerged lower levels. Down those steps and along a narrow hallway was her own bedroom. She wondered if it was still hers or if they'd removed every trace of her; bundled her clothes, torn up her books, stripped her posters from the walls and burned them.

She shut her eyes, telling herself to be strong. This was her grandmother's house, the place where she'd stay whenever her father went away to sea. She'd always understood that he had to go, that his work was too important to be postponed, but somehow it had still felt like abandonment. She would try to lose herself in schoolwork, in seagoing adventure stories, but sometimes the loneliness was overwhelming.

And now he'd deserted her again. Or rather she'd deserted him, which must be why she was standing out here alone, with the neighbours across the street watching through their lowered shutters and her own family sitting inside somewhere, waiting for her to go away.

This was her third attempt to reach them since her return to Frisco, and each time it was the same. She knew someone was home: she could hear the faint thump of music and smell the back-porch barbecue; once she even saw the outline of a figure by the fence, out towards the water. All she wanted was the chance to explain herself. Even if it failed, and it almost certainly would, she wanted to tell her side of the story. But they wouldn't even open the door.

Not for the first time she wished that Kara was here. She'd know what to say. But Kara was gone, swept out during that awful pirate attack and the night-long storm that followed. They'd tried to find them but there were so many beacons to track – by the time the pirates had been driven off more than ninety Mariners had gone overboard – over a search area of almost two hundred square miles. They'd rescued as many as they could but their first priority was returning Cortez to Frisco, Sedna was insistent on that. So after three days they'd reluctantly headed south, hoping beyond hope that the others were still out there. To Cane it just seemed horribly unfair. Kara and her friends had fought to save a city, and were lost to the waves. She had helped to murder thousands but here she was. Unharmed, and alone.

With a sigh she turned away from the door, trudging back along the tree-lined street. The houses here were broad and squat, built to withstand the titanic storms that battered the California coast. She turned into Telegraph Avenue, the thoroughfare bustling with solar-powered people carriers and plexi-frame bicycles, their design unchanged since the Tech Age. Cane remembered asking her father once why this was so, as they scrolled through images of Frisco before the waters rose, before storms flattened the old city and the Mariners raised a gleaming new one from the wreckage.

There are just some things you can't improve, he'd said. *The shape of a boat, or a bicycle, or a pistol. It's our job to seek out the things we can make better, and work as hard as we can to do so. But some things are perfect as they are. Like you, my hurricane girl.* And he'd tickled her on the belly until she fell on the floor, breathless.

A tram rattled past and Cane climbed on, gripping the railing. Her fellow passengers gossiped quietly, the murmur wrapping comfortingly around her. After months surrounded by hungry, resentful Shanty folk, just being around healthy people had come as a shock. Her father had always viewed these people as weak, these stay-at-home Mariners who preferred the safety of Bay life to the thrill of the ocean. But there wasn't room on the Arks for all of them and, besides, there was work to be done here too, a city to run, a civilisation to maintain. Cane felt comforted by their presence, and not for the first time she wondered if she might some day become one of them and forget the call of open water. Now that would *really* annoy her family.

Her time in the Shanties had helped Cane realise how much of what she'd learned growing up was a lie. All through her childhood she'd been told that the Mariners needed to look after their own, to guard their technology, to fear and distrust the mudfoots no matter how helpless they might seem. Now she knew the truth. The Shanty folk were poor, they were desperate, but they were brave and decent too, most of them. They needed help and the Mariners were in a position to give it – and that was all that really mattered.

Cane knew what her father would say: if you gave

them money they'd waste it, if you gave them technology they'd turn it against you. They're like children – they need to be guided. But they weren't children and they weren't fools; they were just people, and they deserved the chance for a better life.

The tram trundled south along the shore and now she could see Frisco itself, pale and gleaming across the Bay. The city shelved down to meet the ocean, tiered streets built to match the vanished old town. But at the foot of the slope the streets continued, out into the water where gleaming towers stood partially submerged and aquatic vehicles plied along sea lanes marked with blinking buoys.

From this angle the city had always reminded Cane of a living creature, some sort of hump-backed prehistoric amphibian with its head in the water, the towers like spikes projecting from its submerged spine. And if this monster had an eye, it would be the Council Chamber – a gleaming plastiglass dome set right on the edge of the city so it was visible from every part of the Bay. At school she'd learned the thinking behind this: the Chamber was made of glass so every Mariner knew that their leaders couldn't hide from them. Here in Frisco, power was transparent.

They reached the waterline and a tunnel opened in front of them, the tram rattling inside, the tracks sloping downward. The walls were clear and through them Cane could make out the shapes of ancient buildings half sunk in the bottom of the Bay, schools of silver fish darting through empty, eroded window frames. Squinting up she could see the shapes of boats on the surface of the water, black hulls with waves trailing behind. Joe would've loved this, she thought, and bit her lip.

The tunnel diverged and they took the westward track, out towards the northern tip of the city. The tram emerged into sunlight, clattering along floating walkways between the towers. Passengers began to disembark, bidding each other farewell, and Cane felt a sudden rush of jealousy. These people were all together, part of a family, a group, the great Mariner project itself. She felt separated from all those things, a stranger, an interloper. A traitor.

She stepped off the tram near Marina Green, a cluster of five or six stubby towers linked by steel bridges. The walkways here were fringed with plant life – hardy coastal shrubs, sedge and gorse. To the west she could see the deep-water docks and two Arks lying in port – the *Neptune* and her sister ship the *Poseidon*. Smaller vessels busied around them like minnows: submersibles and haulage craft unloading and restocking, inspecting and repairing. Beyond, she could make out the rusted span of the Golden Gate Bridge, raised on concrete stanchions, its northernmost tower listing east as it had for well over a century.

Her own residence was in Marina Block Five, known to everyone as the Tower of Lost Children. The name was half a joke – these kids weren't lost, simply left temporarily by parents on oceanic assignment, or in the worst cases orphaned and raised by the community. But to Cane the name felt appropriate: she didn't consider herself a child, not after all she'd seen. But she definitely felt lost.

"Been to see your folks again?"

She stopped by the elevator, turning to see a bearded man smiling at her with earnest concern. Marco wasn't the worst of the guides – there was an older woman called Persephone who had tried every day for a week to get Cane talking. But he could still be a busybody, tilting his head sympathetically as she backed into the lift. "Still won't see you, huh? That's too bad."

"They must've been out," Cane said, reaching for the button. "It's fine. I've got plenty to do with the investigating committee and Academy starting again soon. Probably for the best."

"Well you know where I am, day or night," he said. "You can just say, 'Marco, I'm freaking out. I need to—'"

The doors slid shut in his face and Cane breathed a sigh of relief. Then as the lift ascended she felt a twinge of guilt. The guides were good people and loads of kids benefited from their insights. She just knew that when it came to her, they were out of their depth. She hadn't been left behind, she hadn't lost her parents – well, in a sense she had, but that wasn't the issue.

The truth was that she'd been part of an act of mass murder; she'd stood at her father's side as he killed thousands. She'd even tried to shoot Nate, and however much she wanted to pretend it was an accident, she knew deep down that she'd meant to do it. She was a killer, in thought if not in deed. And she didn't think Marco and his band of eager do-gooders were equipped to help her deal with it.

She unlocked her door with a pass key, shoving it shut behind her. The room wasn't much to look at – a white box containing a bed, a chair and a wardrobe with a single change of clothes. Through glass doors her balcony looked north, past the docks towards the humming hydroelectric plants of San Pablo. She leaned on the railing, picturing herself leaving this place, packing a bag and just walking into the wilderness, never to—

The knock on the door was sharp and sudden.

"Not now, Marco," she called. "I know you're trying to help but I just want to be on my own."

But the knock came again and she sighed, crossing the

room. Maybe he was right to be persistent, maybe she did need someone to talk to. She tugged on the handle and stepped back in surprise.

The man standing there was sturdy and square-shaped, not much taller than Cane herself. His skin was dark and his head was bald, his eyes shining as he smiled at her, exuding warmth and welcome and a hint of apology.

"Well?" he said, holding out his hands. "Don't you have a hug for your Uncle Rex?"

Cane was too startled to refuse, trying not to stiffen as he put his arms around her. Then he let go and edged forward, driving her with him as he pushed into the room. He shut the door and looked around, nodding. "Not bad. Very comfortable."

Rex Cortez had never reminded Cane of her father; he was squat and muscular where John was lithe and streamlined. All they had in common was their accent and their piercing blue eyes. The two men had never been close – in her earliest memories Rex was a distant presence, the kind of uncle who'd show up once in a while, give her a sweet then ignore her. And then six years ago the brothers had fallen out bitterly, and publicly: Rex was trying to get himself nominated to the Council, and had openly criticised John's methods as captain of the *Neptune*. They hadn't spoken since, but it didn't seem to have done Rex any harm: he was defence minister now, and a highly respected member of Mariner society.

"What are you doing here?" Cane managed, blushing as she realised how rude that sounded.

Rex laughed. "I should have come before. I know you've been trying to reach your grandmother and your cousins, but with everything that happened, it's tough. Everyone's so shocked."

"They think I betrayed my father," Cane said flatly. "That I'm a traitor to the family."

Rex frowned. "They said the same of me, at one time. But once they understood, they came around. Cane, that's all this is about. Everyone's trying to understand. Now, I know you've been giving evidence to Councillor Weaver's committee, letting them record your thoughts and memories – that's good, I support that. Your recollections may not chime exactly with what others who served on the *Kraken* have said, but that's OK – memory's a funny thing."

"I've told the truth," Cane said, bristling slightly. "Only the truth."

Rex nodded. "I'm sure you have. And it all helps to establish what your father was trying to achieve, and how it all went so wrong."

"He was trying to invade London," Cane said. "And

it went wrong because people fought back. Even though they were poor and starving they stood up and it still didn't stop him from—"

"All right," Rex cut in. "John was always an extremist. But at least he was trying to do something, wasn't he? To make a change in the world."

Cane kept her eyes on the floor, feeling his hand on her shoulder. His voice was calm and comforting, so similar to the one that had soothed her to sleep all those times.

"Your father may have foundered in deep water, but that doesn't mean you have to," he said. "Cane, your family still love you. They want to see you. They just need to know that you're … that you're still one of them. There's no need for you to swim out here alone, in this darkness."

She lifted her head, looking up into his sparkling blue eyes. "What do they want me to do?"

9

Monuments

The Five's army rumbled along the DustRoad, the sand plume trailing for miles into the baking blue sky. Joe pressed his forehead against the window of the train car and watched the trucks advance, grinding up a shallow hillside of scrub and dry creek beds, the ground shaking and breaking beneath their wheels.

He couldn't help marvelling at the sheer diversity and ingenuity of these mechanised monsters. Some of the vehicles had four wheels, some six, some thirty or more encased inside clattering metal tracks with treads to grip the ground. Some were armoured in steel plate while others were little more than skeletal roll-cages with wheels attached. But each one looked equally unstoppable, surging relentlessly through the barren landscape.

It was their third day on the road and Joe couldn't begin

to guess how many miles they'd covered. Last night they'd camped in a place where the sand was as white as the snow that sometimes fell in the Shanties, great hillocks of it rising around them. He had wanted to run out in it, to slide down those dunes, but Kara wouldn't hear of it. They needed to stay together, she said, and keep their heads down. These were dangerous people, and they couldn't afford to draw attention to themselves.

He could hear her voice from the lounge room now, debating with those men, those Five. Joe still hadn't figured out what the deal was with them – were they identical twins, or whatever it was called when there were five of you? But that didn't seem to be enough, somehow – they were almost *too* alike. It was very disconcerting.

Nate lay in the same position he'd occupied for most of yesterday and all of the day before – face down on the bunk, saying nothing. Joe didn't think he was sleeping – he was just lying there. He hesitated then stepped over, shaking the boy gently.

"I'm going to see if there's breakfast. Do you want to come?"

Nate grunted and shook his head. "I'm fine."

"I'll bring you something, then," Joe said. Then he leaned close and whispered. "And I'll let you know if we find out anything important."

Nate sat up, his eyes red-rimmed. "Great, Joe, you do that. If you figure out how to broadcast to my people over thousands of miles or you suddenly learn how to fly, you come and tell me, OK?"

Joe backed up, trying to think of something to say, anything that might be comforting. But Nate was already turning away, throwing himself back down on the bed and covering his head with a pillow. He was right, of course. So far they'd failed to come up with any way to stop The Five or warn the Mariners. But Joe wasn't ready to give up yet.

As he stepped into the corridor the train car lurched and he grabbed the wall, steadying himself as he made for the lounge in the centre. The Five sat in a row on the red-leather couch, sipping small cups of coffee and facing Kara on the other side.

"This whole business with Cortez," one of them was saying, "his attack on London, it couldn't have come at a better time for us." Joe saw the scar over his eye – this was the one who'd wanted to kill that prisoner.

"We'd been working towards reunification for years," the next joined in. "Talking to war chiefs, presidents, state sheriffs, trying to convince them to end their petty disputes and come together."

"But it was slow-going," another added. "Even with all

the benefits we offer, like our ranch programme."

"Starvation rates in Texas have plummeted under our watch." This was the one with the Morse code birthmark; Joe could see it peeking from under his sleeve. "But it still wasn't enough. They'd gotten so used to fighting each other."

"Then along comes Cortez, and boom!" The last man cracked his knuckles so loudly that it made Joe jump. "Scares the life out of everyone, gets them all running over to our side. They've hated the Mariners for years, now they're scared of them too. And when people get scared, they get angry."

"But why do they hate them?" Kara asked. "What did the Mariners ever do to them?"

"Well, that's the million-dollar question, isn't it?"

"The Mariners have always set themselves apart."

"Hoarding their tech."

"Acting like they're better than everyone else."

"Then three years back there was a disaster."

"Have you heard of wheat blight? It's a disease that attacks crops. Very tricky to fight."

"The outbreak swept through the Midwest. Thousands were starving. Tens of thousands."

"People begged the Mariners for aid."

"And they sent it. Dried seaweed chips and algae powder."

"Tasted like sand."

"But that's what they eat themselves, at sea," Kara explained. "It's portable and nutritious."

"It's disgusting."

"We wouldn't feed it to a pig."

"That made a lot of people very bitter."

"Cortez just tipped things over the edge."

"And the result was that army out there." Scar-eye gestured through the window. "Militias from seventeen different states, all finally agreeing to work together."

"So you're just using the Mariners," Kara said. "You're giving these people someone to hate, so they'll join up and follow you."

Birthmark shifted uncomfortably. "It's not just about that."

"But you've got the general idea," Scar-eye smiled.

"Someone has to unite this shattered nation, Kara," one of his brothers said.

"Someone has to lift America out of the ashes."

"Give the people out here the chance for a better life."

"And what about the ones who lose their lives?" Kara asked. "On your side as well as theirs. It won't be an easy fight, you know."

"Well, perhaps we have a few tricks up our sleeve."

"Something they're not expecting."

Scar-eye flashed a frown. "That's enough."

Footsteps sounded on the upper deck and moments later the door slid aside, a uniformed officer saluting in the entranceway. "Sirs, you asked to be alerted when we were approaching the compound."

The Five looked at one another, rising abruptly. Joe felt a sudden tension in the air.

"Let's take a look."

"See how much the old place has changed."

The man with the birthmark beckoned to Kara. "You can join us if you like. Joe too."

They followed him up a narrow, twisting staircase to the observation deck. The Five were proud of their command centre, but Joe had been on the bridge of a Mariner Ark and this paled in comparison. Pasted to one wall was a map of the continent, a black pin marking what he guessed was their approximate position, a little less than halfway across. Below the map was a table piled with ancient radio equipment and battered computer monitors, all switched off.

But the glass dome overhead gave them an all-round view, and this at least was impressive. They were travelling across an empty plateau ringed by black peaks, the pitted road running in a straight line ahead of them. The Five stood in watchful silence, their eyes fixed on the horizon.

Joe saw a shape in the distance and shielded his eyes.

It was a metal disc, its round face tilted towards the sky, its support struts rooted in the ground. There were several of them, he saw, rising from the plain like statues. At first he couldn't tell how big they were – the landscape was featureless, there was nothing to compare them to. But as they drew closer he realised they were as tall as tower blocks, mighty monuments standing sentinel over this desolate place.

"Let's hope the old man kept them working," one of The Five muttered, and the others nodded.

There were other structures around and below the enormous discs, concrete buildings linked by cracked roadways with grass spiking through. Maybe this was an important place once, Joe thought, the home of some king or president who'd had these statues built in his honour, like the pyramids in India or wherever. The train car passed below one of the discs, its shadow falling over them. It was rusty and windswept but still somehow grand, as though possessed of an ancient power.

They drew to a halt between the buildings and The Five stared down in silence, lost in thoughts Joe couldn't begin to guess. Then as one, they moved toward the steps, striding down and out of the train car. Kara and Joe looked at one another, and followed.

A warm wind swept across the plain as behind them the convoy rumbled to a halt. The Five marched up to a rusty red door, looking at one another almost nervously. Then Scar-eye reached out and knocked, the dull thump sounding hollow in the building beyond.

For a long time nothing moved; there was no sound except the tick of cooling metal and the whisper of the wind. He knocked again and the sound echoed back through the building, rebounding from hard concrete walls.

"Perhaps he's gone," one of the men said.

"Or he's dead."

"Unlikely."

"That old villain could survive a nuclear blast."

"Wait, I heard something."

"Someone's coming."

They fell silent and Joe heard shuffling footsteps on the other side of the door.

"Hello?" a cracked voice called. "Who's there?"

The Five seemed to draw a single breath.

"It's us."

"We've come back."

"Let us in."

There was another tense silence.

"No," the voice said at last. "G-go away, boys. I don't

want to see anyone."

The Five glanced at one another.

"Open up, old man."

"You must've looked out."

"You know we're not alone."

"We can break this door down if we have to."

"Please, Father."

Joe looked at Kara in surprise. They heard the clunk of a lock and the sound of bars being drawn back.

The door creaked open and a wrinkled face squinted up into the light. The man was crooked and white-haired, dressed in a dirty white coat with metallic instruments stuffed in the pockets. His feet were bare and filthy.

"Y-you always refused to say that word," he said, his voice quavering. "You said it was sentimental and incorrect."

"Well, now you're the only one left."

"So maybe it fits."

The old man's lip trembled. "Why are you here? Why have you come back?"

The Five stood over him, their expressions blank.

"The transmission array."

"Is it still working?"

"We need to use it."

The old man spluttered, pushing his spectacles up his

nose. "I haven't powered it up in y-years," he said. "It's on a solar circuit – there's no reason it wouldn't still run, but why do you…"

"Never you mind."

"That's our business."

"We just need to— What was that?"

They jerked suddenly upright, looking past the old man into the building beyond. Joe had heard something too – a faint clang, like a metal door slamming shut.

Scar-eye stepped forward, grabbing the old man by the collar. "Who's in there? What are you hiding?"

The old man kicked as his feet left the ground. "Rats," he wheezed. "Must be … rats. No one … here but … me."

Scar-eye let go and the old man slid to the floor, rubbing his throat.

"You know what'll happen if you lie to us," one of the brothers said.

"Now go and get the power on."

"Get the circuits warmed up."

"We'll join you after nightfall."

They turned, marching back towards the train car. The old man staggered inside and Joe felt a rush of pity.

"You shouldn't feel bad for him." One of The Five had turned back, the one with the birthmark on his wrist. "He did terrible things here. Things you'd barely believe."

"What is this place?" Kara asked. "Did you used to work here or something?"

He let out a long sigh. "In a manner of speaking. We grew up here, you see. This was our home."

Joe looked at the desert stretching on every side, at the strange metal shapes rising from the earth.

"It was a research centre initially," the man went on. "Back in the Tech Age it was called the Very Large Array, a radio telescope built to look into the farthest corners of the universe. That's what these machines are for. They're called radar dishes, used to send and receive information over huge distances, even through atmospheric interference."

Joe felt something chime in the back of his mind, a story he'd been told once. "So that's why you've come here?" he asked. "To use these … dishes?"

The man nodded. "That's right. We're going to send a very important message."

10

The Bedroom

"You really think you can make them work?" Kara asked, looking doubtfully at the steel structures rising around them. "You think you can use these ... radiar things to warn the Mariners?"

"Obviously it's a long shot," Nate admitted, the firelight flickering on his face. "But I did pretty good in electronics class – I know how a radio works. Anyway, this might be our only chance. We have to at least try."

The sun had set behind the mountains and dusk was drawing across the plateau. Inside a circle of trucks a fire had been built, a stack of blazing deadwood where the soldiers gathered as the day's warmth drained into the sand. The train car gleamed in the firelight and, as Kara watched, the door slid wide and The Five emerged, tall in silver-studded suits and brown-leather boots.

117

"If they catch us, that'll be it," she whispered. "They'll lock us up, or worse. No more comfy guest room, no more chances to figure out what their plans are."

"And how's that going so far?" Nate asked, a hint of bitterness creeping into his voice. "All I see is you cosying up to them, acting like you're on their side. You haven't even learned their names."

"I'm not sure they have them," Joe put in. "They call each other brother, and everyone else just calls them The Five. But I actually spotted a couple of little differences between them. The one who told us about the dishes has a birthmark on his wrist, just here. And there's one with a scar over his eye – he's mean, he scares me."

"They all scare me," Nate muttered. "I don't know how you can separate them."

"We could give them names of our own," Joe suggested. "To remind us which one's which. The birthmarked one can be Dash, because it looks like Morse code. And the mean one, let's call him Scar."

"Yes, that fits," Kara said with a shiver. She studied The Five through the flames, seated in a line sipping beer from glass bottles. "The one in the middle should be Grey, because if you look super close he's got a couple of grey hairs, just at the sides here. And the one next to him, he's always cracking his fingers. So let's call him Knuckles."

"What about the last one?" Joe asked. "Does it look to you like his nose got broken once and didn't totally heal up, right?"

Kara nodded. "How about Flatface? Or Punchbag?"

"Boxer," Nate said. "My uncle had a dog called that. It was stupid and dangerous, just like—"

He broke off, hearing shouts across the fire. A fight had started, two soldiers scuffling in the dust while the others stood round and cheered. Kara saw Lynx and the Wildcats among them, laughing as one of the men shoved the other back into the fire and he screeched, batting at his blazing clothes.

But he rose with a knife in his hand, lunging at his opponent. Soon there was blood on the sand.

Kara sat back down, shaking her head ruefully. She'd seen worse most days in the Shanties. But Nate stayed on his feet, looking queasy as the loser's body was dragged away between the trucks.

"These people are awful," he said. "I'll do anything it takes. I don't care if they catch us, we have to warn the Mariners."

One by one the stars came out, prickling the desert sky. Kara remembered what Dash, the birthmarked one, had told her – that the dishes had been used to look at the stars and the planets and the spaces between. She wondered what people had discovered, out there in the dark.

Then Nate put a hand on her arm and she turned. The Five had left their seats by the fire, moving silently towards the concrete building. One tugged the door open and Kara watched as they vanished inside.

Across the fire the Wildcats lay flat on their backs, passing a bottle. But they weren't paying attention to anyone but each other so Kara climbed quietly to her feet, following Nate to the door. They slipped inside, the hinges groaning as Joe pushed it shut, leaving them marooned in darkness.

"Torch," Kara cursed. "Why do I always forget to bring a torch?"

"Like this?" Joe asked, a beam of white light leaping from a tiny flashlight in his hand. "I rescued it from my life jacket before that lion boy stole it. I thought it might come in useful."

The room in which they stood was strewn with debris; there were desks piled against the wall and the floor was littered with paper, all printed with tiny letters and symbols Kara couldn't begin to decipher. On the far side was a door marked AUTHORISED PERSONNEL ONLY, and Joe switched off the torch as they inched through into a long stone corridor. At the far end they could see light and hear voices – The Five, not too far ahead.

"Stay back," Kara whispered. "We can't let them see us."

"But we can't let them get away either," Nate insisted. "I reckon this place is bigger than it looks from outside."

His hunch was soon proved right, as they came to a set of stone steps winding deep into the earth. The voices faded and Nate hurried them along, taking the steps two at a time. At the bottom was another corridor, the wind gusting hollow through steel ventilation shafts. They passed empty offices on either side with more papers scattered everywhere, yellowed and curling. Then suddenly Kara saw movement and grabbed Joe's arm. "Over there, quick!"

The torch beam flashed across cracked plaster and broken furniture, and just as it hit the corner of the room Kara saw a large shape ducking out of sight, a figure in a black coat darting through a second door. "Who's there?" she demanded. "Show yourself!"

"Shush!" Nate hissed. "What if it's The Five? They'll catch us."

"Why would they be creeping around in the dark?" Kara objected. "Anyway it wasn't dressed like them – it had a flappy sort of jacket thing and long hair."

"Remember before," Joe said, "when The Five asked

that old man if there was someone else here? I think he was lying."

"Me too," Kara agreed. "This'd make a pretty good hideout if someone didn't want to be found."

"Well if they don't want to be found, let's not find them," Nate said. "We're here for a reason, remember? We mustn't get distracted."

They returned to the corridor but now they'd lost all sign of The Five – the subterranean bunker was utterly silent. They came to a junction, three corridors branching from the main one. Nate got down on his knees, searching for any sign of The Five's passage. But there was too much debris, piles of rubble and flakes of paint and more scattered papers.

"What do we do now?" he asked. "Split up?"

"Don't be crazy," Kara snorted. "Not with that … whoever it was lurking about. This was your plan, so pick a direction and let's go."

Nate inspected each of the corridors, racked with indecision. "That one," he said at last, indicating the right-hand way. "Look, this sign says B-O-R and I think that's a T, it might have been 'Laboratories'. The transmission array could be nearby."

"That's a lot of mights and could-bes," Kara said. "But sure."

At the end of the hall was a heavy door – they had to work together to haul it open, and when they did a blast of stale air hissed out. A plaque read "Laboratory C – Protective Clothing Must Be Worn", but the place had clearly been abandoned years ago. The floors were tiled beneath layers of dust, the walls stacked with metal tables and wheeled gurneys. In the torchlight Kara saw steel tanks and rubber hoses, trays heaped with surgical tools and bandages. She pocketed some, just in case.

The next room was a storage area, with rows of shelves piled with crates and caskets and containers. Joe jumped back with a shout as two green eyes fell on them, swimming in clear liquid.

The jar was bigger than Kara's head, a pale, embryonic form pressed up against the glass. She saw clawed hands with three fingers each, a toothless mouth and tufts of black hair. The eyes stared lifelessly into the room, as they must have done for decades. Beside it was another jar and another wrinkled shape, and beyond it another.

"Let's get out of here," she whispered shakily. "This is horrible."

They hurried between the shelves towards another door, emerging with relief into a white-walled chamber. Nate shone the torch around, letting out a low whistle of disbelief.

"Just when you thought this place couldn't get any creepier."

Standing in a neat row against the far wall were five small beds, their white sheets turned down. Beside each bed was a table containing a lamp and an empty water glass, and fixed to the headboards were small metal plaques with numbers stencilled on them, counting from 001 to 005.

"I feel like Snow White," Kara said, opening a closet to reveal five white coats hanging above five pairs of shiny black shoes. She unhooked one of the coats – it was too short for her, though not by much. Children had lived here, she realised. Children who had grown up to be men.

"I think we should leave," Joe said. "This place gives me the heebie-j—"

A door clanged. It was followed by a voice in the adjoining corridor, a low, tuneless humming.

Nate looked around in panic. In the back corner a small door stood open and he ran for it, Joe and Kara close behind. Inside was a mirror, a toilet and a sink – but no way out and nowhere to hide. Kara froze in the doorway as the humming grew louder. "I think it's one of The Five."

"I don't care who it is," Nate hissed. "We can't let them see us."

"But if they find us all hiding in here they'll know we were up to something," Kara said. "I'm going to stay and make sure they don't."

"Kara, no!" Nate protested. "They'll suspect something, they'll—"

"Hush!" she ordered and pulled the bathroom door shut, turning just as a tall figure ducked through the far doorway, stopping in mid-hum.

"Kara," he said in surprise, shining a torch on her. "What are you doing here?" In the pale light she could just make out the birthmark on his wrist. Dash, Joe had called him.

Kara gulped and tried to look innocent. "Just … um … having a look round," she said breezily. "The others went to bed but I couldn't sleep. I remembered what you told us, that this used to be a science place. I've always liked science. It interests me."

"Really?" Dash said, lowering the torch. "I assumed Joe was the academic one. You struck me more as a woman of action."

Kara blushed. "Well, a person can be lots of different things, can't they?"

Dash pursed his lips, considering this. "Yes, I suppose they can."

"I saw lots of offices," Kara said. "And the labotter …

125

latobo … the labs. But what's this place?"

Dash looked around. "Haven't you guessed? This was our bedroom. My brothers and me. Look, this was my bed, right on the end. Number five. Last of the litter."

"So your parents were scientists?" Kara asked. "That man, is he really your father?"

"One of them," Dash said. "It's … complicated. We're not like you, Kara. We're not like anyone in the world, as far as we know. We had three fathers, and seven mothers. We're clones."

Kara had heard the word before but she couldn't remember where; in one of Joe's stories most likely. "Our fathers were biologists," Dash went on, "and two of our mothers as well. They took their genetic material and blended it, taking the best from each – one's strength, another's height, another's agility. They were all highly intelligent so they knew we would be too. Then they injected that blended material into five different women – actually more, but some of their attempts failed."

Kara thought of the embryos in the jars and shuddered.

"We were the five that worked, the ones who came out just how they wanted. Five perfect babies. We look the same, sound the same. We even think the same. We are uniquely identical."

"Not quite," Kara said, glancing down at his wrist.

Dash's face reddened and he covered his birthmark with his sleeve. "A tiny deviation. A glitch in the cloning process. It means nothing."

"So what happened here?" Kara asked. "Where did the scientists go? And why did you leave?"

Dash hesitated, then he sat down on the foot of the bed. "Our parents' research was funded by a militia group," he explained. "Part of the old US Army that had gone rogue and founded their own separatist state, down near the Mexican border. Our parents started out making medicines for them but the militia wanted more. They wanted weapons, so we were designed. We were made to be fast and smart, and we were. By age ten we could run a desert marathon, by fifteen we were performing major surgery. The militia didn't need any more convincing. They asked our parents to make an army of us. You see, they had the same ambition we now have, to reunite this continent. But me and my brothers ... well, we couldn't allow it."

He looked up. "Can you imagine it, Kara? We'd been told we were special, that there was no one like us anywhere. Then they said they were going to make more. Hundreds more. Thousands more. Even quicker, stronger, deadlier. We told our parents we wouldn't have it, and we meant it. They resisted – they were more afraid of the militia than they were of us. So my brothers and me, we … dealt with them. We disarmed them, stripped them and drove them into the desert. We had to."

He broke off, biting his lip. "That old man was the only one who found his way back and by then he was too scared to do anything but follow orders. When the militia commanders came to check on their progress we invited them in and served them a special tea that one of my brothers had made, and that was the end of that. We buried the bodies and headed south. Using our parents' research, we designed and sold medicines, built a thriving business. And we used the money to start plantations, schools and military camps from the border right through to the sea. Soon we were ready to start the real work of bringing America together."

"By killing more people," Kara said, and he flushed.

"But that's the way it has to be," he insisted. "The Mariners had their chance to help, we told you that. We're only doing what's necessary."

"That sounds like your brother talking," Kara said. "The one with the scar. You don't seem like a killer to me."

The clone shook his head forcefully. "I told you, we're the same. There is nothing my brothers would say that I would not say, nothing they'd think that I wouldn't

128

think." He got to his feet. "And I must get back, they'll be wondering what's happened to me. I'll just use the bathroom then I'll—"

"No!" Kara said, grabbing his arm. "Wait, I just…" She racked her brain for an excuse, anything at all. "I went in there before. Everything's smashed up. The toilet's broken, and the sink. And it looked like rats were living in there. Big ones."

"That's strange. Who'd smash up a bathroom?"

Kara shrugged, her heart racing. "Well, this whole place is a bit of a wreck, isn't it?"

The clone frowned. "Then I must return to the transmitter array. There was a delay with the uplink but it should've been fixed by now."

"Can I come?" Kara asked. "I got so turned around before, I don't know if I'd be able to find my way back. And this place is pretty spooky."

Dash eyed her uncertainly. "All right, if you have to. But don't tell my brothers you were in this room. I don't think they'd like it."

"But didn't you just say there was nothing they'd think that you…" Kara started, then she saw the distressed look on his face and forced a smile. "Never mind. It'll be our secret."

To her relief they didn't go through the storage room,

turning instead into a low passageway with steel pipes running along the wall. Glancing back she saw movement in the corridor behind her – Joe and Nate, keeping a safe distance. The hallway led to an open steel doorway with harsh electric light streaming from inside. They stepped through and Kara heard voices.

"...only remains to thank you, Madame General, for all your support," one of The Five was saying. "We're going to do great things together, we truly believe that."

Dash cursed under his breath, hurrying to join his brothers. Kara hung back in the shadows. The room was large and circular like the base of a well, its ceiling lost in darkness. Hulks of machinery loomed all around her, leaning together like the mechanical men in those stories Joe liked, the ones that turned into spaceships. The old man cowered by the wall, staring up at his cloned sons as they stood before a bank of monitor screens, their faces lit with a pale synthetic glow.

"Great things indeed," a voice crackled through ancient speakers. "Godspeed, gentlemen."

Peering through, Kara saw a fuzzy image on one of the screens – a woman in a dark green uniform seated in front of a striped red-and-yellow flag. A line of men stood to attention behind her, rifles clutched in their hands. Then the screen went dark.

Dash turned apologetically to his brothers. "I'm sorry, I just went for a look round the old place and I—"

"You made us look like fools," Scar cut in furiously. "We're The Five, not The Four." Then he spotted Kara and his eyebrows shot up. "What is she doing here?"

Kara took a step back. "I was just … exploring."

"I told her a little of our story," Dash said. "How we came to be who we are."

Scar frowned. "What concern is it of hers? And where are her friends? Are they sneaking around somewhere as well?"

"They're asleep," Kara said quickly. "Back in our room."

"That's a lie."

Kara turned, cursing silently. Lynx stepped into the transmitter room, dragging two reluctant figures by their collars. Nate hung his head but Joe stared wide-eyed at the men standing over him.

"I caught them lurking in the corridor," Lynx said. "They were listening."

"We were just…" Nate spluttered. "We only wanted to—"

Without thinking, Kara stepped forward and slapped him. "You *idiots*," she spat. "You told me you were going to bed. What are you doing down here?"

Nate recoiled, clutching his cheek. "But you… Why did…?"

Kara turned back to Dash. "I know how this looks, but I swear I knew nothing about it. I was all by myself when you found me, wasn't I? Tell them, tell your brothers I was by myself."

Dash nodded. "She was on her own. She told me they'd gone to bed."

"She's a liar," Lynx spat furiously. "You can't believe a word she says. Of course they were all in cahoots. They probably thought they could use all this kit to send a signal to the Mariners."

"How stupid do you think I am?" Kara rounded on Lynx. "Look at this stuff, how would we possibly know how to work it? Nate might have thought he had a chance, but why would I risk my neck for the Mariners, the people who attacked my city?" She turned back to The Five. "I swear, I had no part in this. I wouldn't, not after you've been so kind to us. I'm embarrassed, really."

One of the men frowned; Kara could see the peppery streaks in his hair. "So what should we do with them?" Grey asked her. "What would you do, in our place?"

Kara gritted her teeth. "Well, you can't risk them trying something this stupid again, can you? I suppose they'll have to be locked up."

Nate opened his mouth but Joe took his arm, squeezing it hard. The Five looked at one another.

"Lynx, you take them," Dash said. "Put them on the bus and lock them in."

"But what about…" Lynx protested, pointing at Kara. "You can't just…"

"One of us has given you an order," Boxer snapped. "You know what that means."

Lynx sagged, taking hold of Joe and Nate. Kara could see the hurt in the Mariner boy's eyes as they were hauled away into the corridor.

"Well," Knuckles said, cracking his fingers. "At least now we know who we can trust."

"Indeed," Scar said dubiously. Then he leaned close to Kara. "But I'll be watching you."

11

Alcatraz

"We're just trying to understand who was involved, who knew what, and when." Councillor Sedna leaned forward, fixing Cane with a searching stare. "We know you weren't part of your father's inner circle – you didn't attend meetings or make decisions. But you must have seen something, heard something, either on the *Neptune* itself or back here in Frisco before it all started."

Cane scratched her head, pretending to consider the question. The two Mariners seated either side of the councillor were unfamiliar to her, government investigators working with Sedna to get to the bottom of what Cortez did and who supported it.

"What sort of people did your father meet with?" Sedna asked. "Think back. Do you remember anyone in uniform coming to the house? Did he meet with the captains of other ships, other Arks?"

Cane pressed a hand to her forehead. "I don't know," she lied. "I don't remember."

"Your brother, then," Sedna said. "Is there anyone you might have seen him with, anyone who—"

"My brother was good," Cane shot back. "Elroy was good, and he's dead, so leave him out of it."

"He's dead because he followed your father's orders," Sedna pointed out. "He's dead because John Cortez sent his own son to do his dirty work, to explore the tunnels beneath London."

"And then Kara and Joe got caught up in it," Cane shouted, "and now they're gone too, and so's your nephew, and I couldn't save them."

Sedna took a long breath and sat back. "I don't blame you for what happened to Nate and his friends," she said, more gently. "The only thing I'm concerned with is the attack on London. But perhaps we should adjourn for today. We'll be in touch if we need you again."

Cane stood, feeling tired and unsteady. They'd questioned her for hours, asking how her father had reacted to Kara's speech and how things had got so out of hand, all of which she'd answered. Then they'd moved on to her childhood, to her family and everything that happened before, and that was more difficult.

"I do understand, you know." Sedna approached Cane, leaning on her driftwood stick. "The hearings are recorded and as a councillor your uncle has access to the files. I know he's been to see you, more than once."

Cane swallowed. "He... He's been trying to help. Trying to persuade the rest of my family to speak to me. I just want a chance to explain."

Sedna smiled sympathetically. "Of course you do. But if there are things you want to say to me privately, things you don't want recorded, you can come to me. Whether it's about what happened before the attack, or something you might hear now you're back..."

"Don't ask me to spy on my family," Cane said, taking a step away. "Please."

"This is important," Sedna insisted, gripping Cane's arm. "If we don't learn the truth, it could happen again. More could die, more kids like Nate and Joe and—"

"Take your hand off her!"

Cane whipped round to see Uncle Rex striding into the Chamber, his face flushed with anger. "Councillor, you are permitted to question my niece in a public forum, not harass her in private."

Sedna straightened. "The girl seemed upset. I was simply making sure she was all right."

Rex turned to Cane. "Is this true?"

136

Cane hesitated, then nodded. "Councillor Sedna was just being nice. We were talking about Nate, her nephew, the boy who…"

"Yes, of course," Rex said, simmering down. "Terrible shame what happened. My condolences."

Sedna's mouth was a sharp, thin line. "Thank you. We're still hoping they might be found."

"That's good," Rex said, unable to hide the disbelief in his voice. "No sense giving up, is there? But, Cane, you and I have somewhere to be."

The solar-powered car sped down towards the water, the motor whirring softly beneath Cane's feet. The road surface was made of impermeable plastic and when they reached the shore it simply sank beneath them, replaced by two straight rows of reflective buoys. Wings planed from the sides of the car and she felt the wheels tucking in, the door seals tightening as they powered out into Frisco Bay.

"That always gives me a thrill," Rex smiled. "Even after all these years. I don't know if your dad ever told you, but back at the slave camp where he and I grew up we'd sometimes get to drive the trucks, these big old Tech-Age monsters, hauling rice and sugar beet down to the coast. It was hard work – steep roads – you had to keep your hands glued to the wheel. But it beat working in the plantation, getting the lash on your back because you took a moment to catch your breath."

He gestured ahead at the half-submerged towers, at the distant ships, at the sunlight sparkling on the waters of the Bay. "You'll never understand it, Cane. And neither will the councillor back there. You grew up with all this. But me and John… When the Mariners raided the camp, when they saved us and brought us here, we thought it was paradise. Literally, we thought we'd died and gone to heaven. And we made a vow that day to do anything we could to keep this place safe. Anything at all. We've never broken that promise."

He turned to look at her and his eyes were suddenly serious. "I know you thought we were going straight to your grandmother's, but there's something you need to do first. Someone you need to see." He gestured through the front windshield and Cane felt her heart seize.

Alcatraz Island sat low in the water, ringed with a concrete bulwark. The prison on its peak was built of ancient stone, pale and wind-smooth, with barred black windows.

"You just have to speak to him," Rex assured her. "You don't have to agree with him. You don't have to change your mind. You just have to reconnect. And when it's done I'll take you to your grandmother. She's making your favourite, shrimp gumbo and kelp fritters."

"But you and my father hate each other," Cane said, confused. "I thought you hadn't spoken in years."

Rex patted her hand. "I promise I'll explain everything when you're done."

Cane sat still but her mind was racing. The island loomed larger, spiked with security towers and guard emplacements, as dark and foreboding as her thoughts.

Then an automatic sensor was triggered and the wheels swivelled outward, touching down as the road rose to meet them. At the checkpoint a uniformed Mariner scanned Rex's security pass before admitting them into the parking lot below the steep face of the prison.

"I won't come in with you," Rex said. "But here, before I forget." He took Cane's wrist, pressing his own on to it. She felt the storage chip pulse beneath her skin. "He asked us to send him some money, for luxuries you know. Just pass it over when you see him."

Cane climbed from the car, forcing down her doubts. Alcatraz towered over her, a tiered precipice of concrete and steel. She gritted her teeth and started forward.

An automated door swung open to admit her and the officer on the desk looked up. She beckoned Cane through a metal detector that scanned her from head to toe – she saw her outline on the monitor, her chip glowing blue along with the zip of her jumpsuit and the caps of her boots.

On the other side a young prison guard waited, gesturing for Cane to follow him. "Welcome to Alcatraz, Miss Cortez," he said, unable to hide the excitement in his voice. "Usually our visits take place in that secure room over there, but this is a special case. We have to go down to the vault."

He led Cane into an elevator, the doors sliding shut. As they descended the guard smiled nervously, drumming his fingers on the handle of his nightstick. "I have to… I don't mean to be rude but I wanted to ask… Is it true you were there? In London? During the battle?"

Cane looked at him. "Yes, I was there. Why?"

The young man beamed. "It must've been something. I mean, I read about it on the newsfeeds, but to actually be there… I heard they're planning a movie. I wonder who'll play you?"

Cane tried to speak but nothing came. The lift doors slid wide and she stepped out, her head pounding in the harsh electric light. They marched along a stone corridor lined with ancient, empty cells. In the distance she heard cries and clanging metal.

"Just wait in here," the guard said, showing her into a small interview room. Cane took a seat, trying to steady her heartbeat. There were cameras pointed at the table and metal loops embedded in the concrete floor. For a moment all was quiet, just the hiss of the pipes. Then the far door opened and her father was standing there, in a white jumpsuit with his hands cuffed in front of him.

The guard nudged him forward, ushering him into the chair opposite Cane and locking his chains to the floor. Then he retreated to the back of the room and stood against the wall, watching keenly.

John Cortez was thin, that was the first thing Cane noticed. He'd never been a big man but now his cheeks were gaunt, his eyes lurking deep in his sallow face. He placed his hands on the table, as close to Cane as the chains would allow. The webs between his fingers hung slack.

Then she looked up, meeting his gaze, and suddenly the prison dropped away, the walls and the island and all of it, and they were father and daughter again, just sharing each other's company.

"I wanted to say I'm sorry," Cortez began. "I'm sorry you got caught up in … well, in all of it. I should have kept you away, I realise that now. You weren't ready. But I only did what I thought was right, Cane. And I still love

141

you more than anything – I hope you can believe that."

Cane dropped her eyes, feeling her pulse throbbing in her temples.

"I feel stronger than I did," Cortez went on. "Those last days, everything was so … intense. With Elroy and Redeye and Kara, and that last mad rush to prepare. I'm calmer now. Back to the man I was before they took my son. I still miss him, though. Every minute."

"So do I," Cane said. "I… I miss you, too. I miss all of us being together."

Cortez reached for her, straining against his chains. "We'll be together again, I promise. Not Elroy, not him, but you and me. There's still so much to do, so much to be achieved." He lowered his voice. "I mean it, Cane. You'll see. When I get out of here, I'll—"

Cane jerked back. "When you get out? Father, you know that's never going to happen. After what you did … you're going to die in here."

Cortez pursed his lips. "Not necessarily. You never know what the future will bring."

Cane stumbled to her feet, her heart racing. "What are you up to? Are you planning something? Are you plotting again? You'll get yourself killed this time, you'll—"

"Stop," Cortez said, and the warmth was suddenly gone from his voice. "I mean, there's no need to get yourself worked up. Sit back down."

Cane shook her head. "No. I can't stay here. I should never have come. It was a mistake." She looked at the guard. "Can you let me out?"

The young man crossed towards her but Cortez held up a hand. "If you must leave, I understand. But didn't Rex give you something for me? A little spending money?"

Cane glanced at the guard and he nodded quickly. She touched wrists with her father, his skin rough and warm. She felt the chip pulse then she turned away, marching from the room.

She huddled low in her seat as they crossed the Bay, cloud shadows shifting on the grey water. Uncle Rex steered into the Berkeley sea lane, gesturing south towards the shipyards where a huge black submarine lay in dry dock, engineers and construction workers swarming over it.

"There she is," Rex said proudly as Cane recognised the giant carcass of the *Kraken*. "The vessel my ministry commissioned to defend Frisco. The one I stole and gave to your father. The one those mudfoots crippled and that we had to drag a thousand miles back for repairs."

"The disagreement between you," she said. "It was all an act, wasn't it?"

"Of course," Rex smiled. "Our dispute had to be nasty,

and it had to be public. The Council needed to have no doubt where my loyalties lay. But in truth, they were always with my family, with my brother. And they always will be."

They rolled up on to dry land, turning into the long, tree-lined street and pulling up behind the house on the shore, the half-sunk one with the driftwood door. Through the kitchen window Cane could see her grandmother stirring a pot, her spectacles fogged by the steam. Suddenly she reached a decision.

"I don't want this," she said, forcing the words out. "I lied to Councillor Sedna for you, I kept the family out of it. But whatever my father is planning, whatever you're going to do, I don't want to be involved."

Rex smiled. "Oh, child, it's much too late for that. You're already involved."

Cane gritted her teeth. "I mean it. If you force me, I'll go to someone. I'll tell Sedna, I sw——"

Her uncle's hand moved so fast it was a blur, locking around Cane's wrist. His face was suddenly close to hers, his mouth tight, his eyes hard. "If you say anything to anyone, you're done," he spat. "I don't care whose daughter you are, we will end you, child."

He let go and Cane scrambled back, pressing up against the door of the car, breathing hard.

But Rex just chuckled softly. "Come on, you look like you've seen the ghost of Davy Jones and his monkeys. If you do as you're told, you'll be fine. Better than fine. London wasn't the only scheme your father and I came up with, you know. Wait till you hear about Plan B." He clapped her on the shoulder. "Let's get inside. You know your grandma hates to be kept waiting."

12

Fort Coronado

The yellow bus rattled along a stony track between rows of slender pines, trailing The Five's army like a pebble in the wake of a landslide. Inside, the air was choked with dust, powdery clouds swirling in the beams of light slanting from bullet holes in the walls and windows. Joe sat hunched on the frontmost bench, his hands cuffed in front of him, peering through a crack in the steel plate and wondering how far they'd come and how far they had left to go.

For two days and nights he and Nate had been confined to this rolling prison, sleeping on the benches and feeding on scraps. He still had the metal shard he'd found in the dust that first night, and they'd been taking it in turns to try to pick their cuffs, so far without success. But where would they go, even if they did escape? They'd left the desert behind but this new place seemed almost worse: a forbidding forest like something from a fairy tale, no doubt crawling with bandits and witches and man-eaters both human and animal.

There was a sudden roar outside the bus and Joe jerked upright. But it was just a car, Leo's hulking off-roader, black smoke gushing from the exhaust. The boy gripped the wheel, smirking as he drew alongside. "Hey, Lynx," he shouted. "How are the kids? Told 'em any good bedtime stories?"

"Get bent, Brad," Lynx retorted, jerking the wheel sideways, the bus lurching wildly. But Leo was too fast; he laughed as he hit the accelerator, leaving a cloud of fumes in his wake.

"Some friends," Lynx muttered bitterly, shifting gears. "Like I chose to play nursemaid to you two dweebos."

Nate snorted. "It's your own fault. If you hadn't betrayed us to The Five in the first place…"

"Betrayed you?" Lynx cut in. "I never owed you anything. I owe The Five *everything*."

"Why?" Joe asked. "Why are you so loyal to them?"

Lynx's eyes narrowed. "What do you care?"

Joe shrugged. "Your friend said to tell us a story. How about that one?"

Lynx hesitated, then sighed. "I guess it can't hurt. Truth

is, I wasn't much older'n you when they found me. I was living on the streets down in El Paso, just one in a million lost kids. The Five put the word out they were going to have auditions – they were looking for reliable folk to carry shipments across the state. I was the youngest in the room but I didn't let it phase me. Then this big guy starts making a fuss, saying he didn't know they were hiring little kids. I didn't even talk back, I just went up and punched him right in the … well, you can guess where. The Five thought it was hilarious. I got hired on the spot."

The smuggler smiled wistfully. "I paired up with Brad that first day. His people were scrap traders so he already had a car. He'd drive and I'd run defence in case we hit trouble. And there was plenty of that, believe me. The stuff we were carrying was the best – aspirin, insulin, Ventolin – everybody wanted it. Leona – Tigress – she came on soon after. She was boss of her own little outfit north of Shreveport, tried to snatch our merchandise. It obviously didn't work out. But we liked the way she drove so I asked the bosses to let her join up. That was when they started calling us Wildcats because we never let our prey get away. We were the best and they gave us anything we wanted. New cars, fine food, you name it. They put their complete trust in us, in *me,* and in return I— What in boot hill's *that?*"

Joe ducked instinctively as something soared above the bus, emitting a deafening roar like a speedboat engine. The convoy slowed as the winged shadow passed over, men shielding their eyes and staring up in disbelief. The flying machine banked in mid-air, soaring back towards them.

"An airplane," Nate said in a hushed voice. "I don't believe it."

The plane was little more than a steel frame with stubby wings poking out, propeller whirring as the engine gushed grey smoke. At the back was a large fin with smaller wings branching from it, and poking from the underbelly were a pair of chunky rubber wheels. A single occupant sat hunched in the exposed cockpit, peering down through plastic goggles.

"My teacher said all the flying machines were gone," Joe said. "Not enough petrol to keep them going."

"Looks like they've stripped this one down," Lynx observed. "Maybe it's light enough to run on chem fuel."

The little plane descended, lower and lower until it was almost skimming the tops of the trees. It kept sinking and Joe cried out, convinced it was going to crash.

Then suddenly the forest fell away and they were driving along the edge of a vast hole in the ground, so wide he could barely see the other side. The walls were sheer and craggy, and in the depths he could make out stone spires banded with lines of coloured rock. There were trees down there too, and the shimmer of water in the valley bed.

"It's a canyon," Nate said in astonishment.

"The Grand one," Lynx told them. "You can kinda see where it got the name."

Joe nodded breathlessly. "I hope we don't fall in."

The trucks sped along the track, sending sand and pebbles cascading over the canyon's edge. The plane rose beside them, keeping level. Joe watched it keenly.

"I wonder where it came from?"

Lynx gestured ahead. "I'm going to hazard a guess and say right there."

Joe lifted his gaze and gulped. A massive structure clung to the canyon's lip, rising like a beached battleship. It reminded him of the Tower of London, high walls of corrugated steel surrounding a courtyard and a stocky central turret. Uniformed gunmen stood on the fort's outer ramparts, their rifles trained as the convoy approached.

"What is this place?" Nate asked. "What are we doing here?"

Lynx shrugged. "It's none of my business. Which means it's certainly none of yours."

The convoy braked, drawing up outside a set of huge spiked gates made from whole pine trunks lashed with rope. The flying machine made a final pass then it descended behind the ramparts. Nate watched it thoughtfully, leaning close to Joe and talking in a whisper. "You know, if we had an airplane we wouldn't have to worry about outlaws or cannibals. We could just fly straight to Frisco."

Joe eyed him doubtfully. "How would we work it? Do you think it's easier or more difficult than a submersible?"

Nate shrugged. "It couldn't hurt to look, could it? If we got the chance."

Joe bit his lip. "I don't think Kara would like it."

Since the radar station they'd only set eyes on her once, sitting by the fire in conversation with one of The Five. Joe had tried to get her attention but she wasn't looking his way – in fact, she seemed to be making an effort not to look at them at all.

Nate touched his cheek resentfully. "I don't really care what she likes."

Joe sighed. "You know why she hit you. She had to convince them, so they'd keep trusting her. She didn't mean to hurt you."

"Well, it felt like she did," Nate said. "It felt … personal."

"Only to you," Joe said. "And only because... Well, because you like her. You do, don't you? I know you think it's a secret but I'm not stupid."

Nate flushed. "I don't know what you're talking about. Me and Kara are friends. Or at least we used to be." He gazed up at the crenellated ramparts and the soldiers standing guard. "But if the opportunity comes, we should take it. I want to get a closer look at that machine."

"Welcome to Fort Coronado," Dash said, gesturing through the train car's observation dome at the steel fort rising over them. "Not that it looks very welcoming, I admit."

"Why have we come here?" Kara asked. "Are these your people too?"

Dash frowned. "Yes and no. These are the headquarters of the Arizona Brigade, one of the oldest and most powerful militias on the continent. They have something we need. Something that'll help us in our fight against the Mariners."

Kara looked at the clone but his face was expressionless, his eyes dark. "It won't be long now, will it?" she asked softly. "Until we reach the border. Until the ... the war. Look, we can still stop this. I know you have doubts about it all. We could talk to your brothers and—"

"I told you," Dash said firmly. "My brothers and I are in complete agreement. On this. On everything."

Kara fell silent. She couldn't risk pushing him. Not yet.

She'd spent almost all her time with Dash in the days since the bunker, talking about the past and the future, telling him of the Shanties and hearing stories about his childhood. She'd been trying to figure out why he was special, what set him apart from his brothers besides his birthmark. Perhaps she could use it somehow, split him off from the rest, get him thinking for himself.

But in the process she'd discovered something unexpected. Every so often the others would join them, chiming in with their own recollections of life in the bunker. And as they spoke, Kara had started to notice differences between them – subtle at first, but more and more obvious the better she got to know them. Despite appearances, each of The Five was unique.

Knuckles had a sarcastic streak; he laughed at everyone, even his brothers, sometimes so subtly that they didn't know they were being mocked. Grey was the calm one; when disagreements arose, his was the deciding voice. Boxer was full of fire; he would arrange sparring matches with soldiers from the army, fights that he invariably won. And he was absolutely devoted to his brother Scar, who Kara now knew was the worst

153

of them: ruthless, sly and vengeful.

"Impressive, isn't it?"

Kara jumped as Scar appeared at her side. "These are tough people," he said admiringly. "Let's hope they still want to buy what we came to sell."

"Come, brother," Knuckles said, joining them, "I'm sure your natural charm will have its usual effect."

"We brought what they asked for," Grey pointed out. "They've no reason to refuse us."

"And if they try," Boxer growled, "we'll soon set them straight."

With a creak, the gates of the fort began to swing open, cogs turning and counterweights descending. Inside was an enormous courtyard with a sandy floor and in the centre, that squat, reinforced tower. A man in a peaked cap waved the train car forward and Scar gave the order to advance.

The soldiers on the rampart turned, keeping the train car in their sights. There were many more in the courtyard, some sparring with sticks or rifles, others just watching silently as the fleet of trucks drew slowly into the stockade. They were all uniformed, all armed and all relatively young, Kara noticed – where were the old folks and the kids? Maybe there was another encampment nearby for civilians.

The flying machine had landed on a strip of earth close to the edge of the canyon, its propeller clattering to a stop. Looking past it, Kara saw that the outer rampart didn't completely surround the courtyard – there was a gap in one side where the wall met the ravine, and on the edge was a winch, and mules strapped to a winding wheel. Perhaps there was more to this place than met the eye.

The train car shuddered to a halt and a door in the fort's central tower swung open. Men marched out, raising trumpets and blowing a brisk fanfare. They were followed by a stocky, steel-haired figure in a green uniform, and as she lifted her head Kara recognised the woman she'd seen on the screen back in the bunker.

"That's our cue," Knuckles said, leading his brothers down to the door of the train car. He reached for the handle but Scar held up a hand, looking back at Kara.

"There's no place for her. These are private negotiations."

Dash frowned. "But I thought—"

"They're expecting to meet The Five," Scar said. "Not The Five plus friend. She stays here."

Kara watched from the doorway as the clones greeted their host, shaking hands in turn. Scar gestured to a pair of trucks parked close to the train car – the same oval-

155

shaped tankers that Lynx and the Wildcats had delivered from the coast. The General nodded her appreciation then they all moved inside, the door swinging shut behind them.

In the courtyard all was quiet, the local militiamen eyeing their counterparts from other states, sizing each other up. As the sun sank the soldiers built a fire and gathered round it, drinking and throwing dice. Kara saw Lynx and the other Wildcats among them, roasting a brace of furry creatures. The bus was parked close by but Lynx barely glanced at it, too busy laughing at some story Tigress was telling. It was fair enough, Kara thought as she headed down the corridor and climbed into her bunk. The boys wouldn't try anything tonight, not with all those soldiers around.

She still felt bad for slapping Nate. She'd panicked, and he'd paid the price. It had worked, she reminded herself. The Five still trusted her and that was vital. But she kept remembering the look in his eyes, so hurt, so betrayed. And she didn't like what it said about herself, that she'd resorted so quickly to violence. That old anger was still inside her, ready to rise up at a moment's notice.

She woke suddenly just before dawn, sitting up in sleepy confusion. There'd been a tap on the window and she lifted the blind, peering out. Two small figures huddled in the shadows, gesturing excitedly. Kara's heart sank.

She slipped noiselessly along the hallway, hearing soft snores on either side. She peered out cautiously; in the light of the guttering fire she could see the Wildcats sprawled in the dust, while beneath the stone tower a pair of Arizona guardsmen sat smoking. But they weren't looking her way so she crept down, hurrying to the rear of the carriage.

"What are you *doing*?" she hissed, startling them. Joe and Nate jerked round and she heard a muffled rattling. "Wait, are you still in handcuffs?"

Joe nodded. "We tried to pick them but we couldn't. We thought you might be able to help."

He held out a small sliver of metal, raising his wrists expectantly.

"First you tell me what's going on," Kara said. "And it had better be good."

Nate flushed. "The thing is…" he said, then stopped.

Joe frowned. "Nate was just…" he started, then he broke off as well.

"Say it," Kara growled.

Joe gestured towards the edge of the canyon. "You see that airplane? We're going to steal it and fly away."

Kara struggled to find the words, but they wouldn't come.

"We're just going to take a look, for starters," Nate said. "If the controls are too complicated we'll go back to the bus. But we have to try. In that thing we could reach Frisco in no time."

Kara felt a wave of frustration. "Look, I get it," she said, as calmly as she could manage. "You want to warn your people. Time's running out and you're feeling desperate. But this is ridiculous, Nate. You need to go back, right now, before Lynx notices you're gone."

"Or what? You'll hit me again?" Nate faced her bitterly. "I don't think you care about the Mariners at all. I think you've made friends with The Five and now you want them to win. You think because their people are poor and hungry like the Shanties, that gives them the right to attack whoever they want."

"You're wrong," Kara insisted through gritted teeth. "Yes, I can see The Five's point about the Mariners not doing enough to help, and I'm still pretty angry with them for not stopping Cortez. But I don't support The Five storming into Frisco – how could you think that? A real chance will come, I swear. I'm already working on it, trying to persuade Dash to—"

"Who goes there?"

Kara whipped round, blinking as a torch flicked on, lighting up their startled faces. A guard had rounded the

158

train car just a few feet away; he was barely more than a boy, wearing a green Arizona uniform. "Who are you?" he demanded. "What are you doing?"

Kara drew herself up. "I'm, err, one of The Five's advisors," she said. "I'm just getting up early to … to fetch them some breakfast. These are the cooks."

Nate smiled awkwardly and Joe gave a little wave. There was a rattle of steel and the guard looked down. "Why has he got handcuffs on? What's really g——"

Kara lunged, slamming into him shoulder first. The torch flew from the guard's hand, shadows leaping as it rolled across the sand.

"Go," Kara hissed, looking back at Nate and Joe. "Now!"

"Not without you," Joe protested.

"Run!" she yelled as the guard seized her arm, twisting it. She cried out in surprise then she swung with her free hand, packing all her frustration into her fist and feeling a grim satisfaction as it made contact. The guard fell on his back and Kara advanced on him. All around she could hear muffled shouts as the fort began to come awake.

Joe ran for the edge of the canyon, Nate hard on his heels. Behind them he could hear Kara scuffling with the guard, followed by the sound of voices and doors slamming.

They darted between a pair of jeeps, startling a sleeping mule that whinnied and tottered to its feet. The little plane stood out in the open and Joe made for it, grabbing the steel frame with his cuffed hands and scrambling up into the cockpit.

Nate climbed into the pilot's seat, studying the rusty control panel. To Joe's surprise it had far fewer buttons than the submersible they'd driven, just two rows of switches and a black plastic handlebar, like a steering wheel with no top or bottom.

"Propeller, propeller," Nate muttered as gunfire sounded from the ramparts. He turned a key and the engine began to rumble, the prop turning, picking up speed. "Good start," he said. "And this must be how you control it."

He grabbed the bar and pulled it towards him, the flying machine juddering, the propeller whirring faster. Through the steel-mesh floor Joe could see rubber wheels turning as the plane rolled forward, angling towards the rim of the canyon. He squeezed on to the seat beside Nate as men converged on them from all corners of the courtyard, yelling and firing. But most of their shots missed – the flying machine's frame was so skeletal that the bullets passed right through.

They began to pick up speed, dust rising beneath the

wheels. But the canyon's rim was getting close now and Nate tugged desperately on the control bar. "I don't think we're going fast enough," he shouted. "We need more power but I don't know how!"

They reached the edge of the canyon and the plane tilted sickeningly. Nate wrestled with the controls as they tipped on to a steep, rocky slope, the wheels bouncing over piles of scree. Then the ground dropped away and Joe saw nothing beneath them, just a long drop to the canyon floor.

The wind rose and the plane bucked, riding an updraft but still descending. Then Nate flicked another switch and suddenly the engine seemed to kick in, the propeller doubling its speed. They began to climb, up into the churning air.

"Must have been some kind of fuel pump," Nate said. "Either way, it worked."

As they soared out over the canyon, Joe could see the treetops far below and the narrow band of the river. For a moment it was almost peaceful, the sky paling around them as colour soaked back into the world.

Then he heard gunfire and jerked round. The soldiers on the precipice were out of range now, just wasting bullets. But something else caught his eye and he grabbed Nate's arm. "Look!"

Kara stood in the shadow of a tall truck right on the edge of the canyon, waving both her arms. As Joe watched, she began to sweep her hands outward in a gesture of dismissal. "I think she's telling us to go," he shouted. "She wants us to leave her. But we can't, can we?"

Nate looked back and Joe could see the struggle behind his eyes. The light was rising in the east, above the dark line of the forest. Nate lowered his gaze, scanning the cockpit floor. He reached down and grabbed something – a length of rope. He shoved it into Joe's hands then he hauled on the control bar, the flying machine banking steeply. "Either we all go," he said, "or none of us does."

The soldiers watched in disbelief as the plane circled back towards the stockade, dropping as it came. Wrestling with his handcuffs, Joe tied the rope to the sturdiest-looking strut and gripped it, poised.

As they drew closer he happened to glance down at the cliffside below the fort and was amazed by what he saw. A series of caves had been burrowed into the rock, linked by rope walkways. He saw faces peering out, children and parents and goats and dogs, watching as the flying machine swept overhead.

Then the ground sloped up to meet them, the ramparts rising ahead. Joe saw a woman in uniform screaming orders, men sprinting to obey. The Five emerged from the train car, clad in identical black-silk pyjamas. But none of them seemed to have spotted Kara on the canyon's edge – they were too preoccupied with the plane itself.

She watched them come, shaking her head incredulously. Joe grinned and dropped the rope, the loose end trailing above the scree slope. Kara darted for it, hands outstretched. As Joe watched she snatched, missed, and snatched again. This time she caught hold, wrapping both hands tightly around. The plane dipped but only for a moment, Nate pulling hard on the control bar.

"Take us up!" Joe shouted. "We've got her!"

Nate nodded and the plane began to lift, struggling with the added weight. The ramparts rose ahead of them, but Joe was sure they were going to make it. He looked down to see Kara climbing the rope, the wind from the propeller battering her face. Then something moved beneath her, a figure leaping from the shadows, bounding on to the roof of the bus.

Joe gave a cry as Lynx sprang, both arms clasping around Kara's legs. Kara tried to kick but Lynx's grip was too tight. And now the plane was dropping again, the weight dragging them back below the level of the battlements. The engine whined and Joe could taste scorched chem fuel.

Lynx clung to Kara as she dangled from the rope, staring helplessly up at Joe. He saw the decision in her eyes as she made it, the look of resignation. And before he could protest she had dropped, plummeting to the courtyard floor, landing with Lynx in a cloud of dust.

Nate looked down in horror. "She let go!"

"She had to," Joe shouted back. "What do we do?"

Nate bit his lip. "Someone needs to warn my people," he said, seizing Joe's hand and placing it on the control bar. "Just follow the sun. Keep going west and you'll find them."

Joe shook his head. "No, wait, don't—"

"I can't leave her," Nate said. "You were right."

And he scrambled from the seat, and jumped.

He landed hard on the battlements, sprawling flat on his back. Joe saw armed men closing in, the Mariner boy raising his hands as they approached. Then he forced himself to turn away, gripping the control bar as the plane rose into the grey light of morning.

13

Wildcat Rodeo

Once the flying machine was in the air, Joe found it quite a simple task to keep it there – all he had to do was hold the control bar steady and watch out for tall trees. By the time the sun was up he'd left both fort and forest far behind, keeping the light at his back and following the westward shadows. The fuel tanks were full and there was a spare canister tucked behind the seat, along with a bottle of water. His hands were still cuffed and he had no food; the few scraps they'd stashed last night had been in Nate's pocket. But hopefully it wouldn't be long before he reached the Mariners.

He tried to remember the last time he'd been separated from Kara for more than a day, but he couldn't. She'd always been there, watching his back, keeping him out of trouble. Now he was alone in hostile territory, and she was back there facing The Five. The urge to turn around was so strong at first that he almost broke, but he just had to picture Nate's face and remember his words – *Someone needs to warn my people.* It was all up to Joe.

Below him the dry brown country stretched to the horizon, utterly silent, utterly dead. Broken highways followed their ancient courses and in empty towns the shattered houses were arranged in vast grids, the streets piled with rubble and refuse. Vehicles lay strewn, the paint peeling back like skin to reveal the rusted carcasses beneath. Some had wheels, some wings, some sat on straight rails that ran for miles upon miles, like seams stitching the frayed land.

Birds drifted by, silver-black ravens and brown eagles, mirrored eyes fixed on the flying machine as it made its way through the hot, rising air. Herds of wild horses thundered over the plains, streaming like water through rocky canyons. And on the banks of a shallow river he saw a cluster of triangular tents, smoke drifting from a cookfire in the centre of the camp. People pointed and dogs barked furiously as Joe passed overhead, waving until they were out of sight behind him.

Kara crouched in the dust, her hands cuffed in front of her. The sun blazed and the air stank of hot metal. Thirty or more trucks had been arranged into a ring, forming a large enclosure. The soldiers sat on roofs and hoods, knocking back cups of home-brewed beer and waiting for the fun to start.

They had left Fort Coronado not long after Joe, the army's ranks swelled by two huge black lorries, twenty assault vehicles and over four hundred armed men from the Arizona Brigade. On The Five's orders Kara and Nate had been chained in the bus, a captive audience for Lynx to gloat over. But Kara knew it was just the start – they'd have to be properly punished for trying to escape and for helping Joe. Scar wouldn't let it go, not this time.

As the sun reached its peak, the convoy had rumbled to a stop, pulling off the DustRoad on to a patch of dead land overlooked by a huge, ruined church. Lynx had dragged Kara out, ignoring Nate's feeble protestations. Now she was chained on the edge of this huge circle of trucks, wondering what form her punishment was going to take.

In the centre of the enclosure was a stack of wood and brush and, as she watched, a man came forward with a canister, drenching it in chem fuel. Then she heard laughter and saw Nate being pushed into the ring, stripped to the waist with a rope around his neck. Lynx tugged him forward like a dog, leading him to the woodpile and tying him to a post in the middle. His mouth moved but Kara couldn't hear his words – he was too far away and there was too much noise from the crowd.

Behind her the train car's door slid open and Scar stepped down, giving a brisk wave. The crowd cheered, drumming on the hoods of their vehicles as his brothers followed – Grey and Knuckles and Boxer. Kara waited for Dash but there was no sign of him. She felt her mouth go dry.

Scar strode over, crouching with his face just inches from hers. He took hold of the chain between Kara's wrists, unlocking her cuffs with a silver key. "If you thought my brother was going to save you, you're very much mistaken," he said, a smile playing around his lips. "He couldn't even bring himself to watch. He was always the weakest of us, you know. Even when we were boys."

"I thought you were all the same," Kara said. "How could one be weaker?"

"Every litter has its runt," Scar spat. "Our situation is … complex. We are the same but we are also different. We are many but we are also one. I wouldn't expect a child like you to understand."

Hearing scattered laughter, Kara looked out across the circle. Lynx had struck a flame, lighting the wick of a short candle and placing it between Nate's bare feet.

When it burned down, the fuel would catch and the pyre would go up.

Lynx glanced at Kara, flashing a silver-toothed smile and retreating from the arena. Kara got to her feet. "I may be a child," she told Scar. "But I've beaten bigger men than you."

The clone laughed. "It's one thing taking on men," he said. "Try beating machines."

And he gave her a shove into the circle, hard and unexpected.

Kara stumbled, skidding on to her knees. The crowd hooted, banging and hollering. Every eye was on her as she picked herself up, brushed herself down. Scar took his seat beneath a canvas awning with his brothers. Boxer passed him a beer and he nodded gratefully.

Kara advanced into the enclosure. Nate hung from the pole some distance away, his eyes pleading as the candle burned. Silence fell, the anticipation building. Then Kara heard the rumble of engines, two – no, three – of them, amplified in the stillness. She started to run, but she already knew what was coming.

The Wildcats roared from a gap in the trucks, soldiers scrambling clear as they shot into the arena. Lynx cut right around the central woodpile while the others broke left, rocketing towards Kara. She froze. Which way to run? All she could hear was the din of their engines; all she could see were the reflections from chrome hoods and wheel rims flashing in her eyes and making her dizzy.

Then they were on her and she ducked aside – too late. Tigress's orange-striped roadster clipped her, spinning her into the dust. Kara rolled on her back and Leo roared over her, the rumbling tailpipe inches from her nose. She coughed, staggering up in time to see Lynx circling in, the sleek, low-roofed vehicle the same colour as the dust beneath its wheels.

Again Kara tried to leap clear but the car was moving too fast. It struck her and she rolled over the hood, briefly coming eye to eye with Lynx as the wheels twisted, throwing her clear. She bounced and spun, bruised and blinded as she came to a skidding stop back on the edge of the circle.

The crowd screamed their approval, punching the air and shouting, "Lynx! Lynx! Lynx!" Kara dragged herself up, blinking the dust from her eyes. Nate looked at her in panic, his mouth working soundlessly, the flame still flickering between his feet.

Then she saw Leo powering towards her, his hulking, steel-topped monster tracking the very edge of the circle, forcing onlookers out of his path. He grinned over the steering wheel, teeth bared as he closed in. Tigress was

170

approaching from the other direction, aiming to cut Kara off if she tried to run. But she ran anyway, putting herself right in harm's way. The two vehicles screamed towards her, leaving her nowhere to go, no way to escape. Except one.

She faked left then leapt as high as she could, her foot striking Tigress's speeding hood, the impact vaulting her forward into the circle. Both drivers were confused; the cars slammed against one another at high speed, metal twisting and tyres popping as they juddered to a halt. Kara heard the hiss of steam as she dropped to the earth and sprinted.

Again the crowd roared, some in dismay, others in surprise and excitement. Below the woodpile the candle was still burning, but now she knew she was going to make it. Nate struggled against the ropes, his eyes blazing with reflected fire.

Then Kara saw something in the corner of her eye and glanced aside, just for a moment. A figure stood in the crowd, taller than the rest and dressed in a long black coat. Why had he drawn her attention, what had made her look his way? Then he pulled back his hood and she almost skidded to a stop. He had a bandage around his eyes, his pale face framed by long, greasy hair. Kara felt her heart seize, her mind rolling over, her pace slowing.

Lynx's car screamed out of nowhere, slamming Kara sideways and sending her flying. She skidded on her back, her skin scraped raw, the breath knocked out of her. She gasped air, coughed dust, dragging herself up. She looked for the dark figure but he was gone, an hallucination, or a coincidence. It was impossible, impossible – it couldn't be him.

There was a quiet *whump* and a wave of heat hit her.

Nate screamed as the flames rose around him. Kara ran, pounding through the dust. Lynx steered for her but Kara dodged, feeling the car glide past. The crowd bellowed.

Kara reached the woodpile, covering her face as another pool of chem fuel caught, singeing her eyebrows and making Nate howl. She tried to reach him, turning as she heard a rumble behind her. Lynx had U-turned in the dust and was hurtling back, closing fast. If the car knocked her into the flames, she'd be badly burned. If she retreated, Nate could die.

Thinking quickly, Kara grabbed a blazing plank, spinning and tossing it as hard as she could, seeing it twist end over end towards the dust-coloured car. Lynx tried to steer clear but the board slammed into the windshield, exploding in a spray of sparks. Lynx lost control, skidding wildly.

Kara ran into the flames. Nate was half conscious, his skin turning red, his hair smoking. She tugged at his bonds but the knots were too tight. She grabbed another piece of wood, feeling her fingers burn as she pressed it down on the rope. String by string it came loose.

The rope snapped and Nate fell into her arms. Kara held him around the waist as they staggered clear. She could smell her own hair burning, feel blisters on her feet and hands. Nate dropped to the sand as the soldiers howled and pounded, making Kara's head spin.

Then suddenly the crowd fell silent and she heard the rumble of an engine coming closer. The car's windshield was patterned with spider cracks but Lynx leaned from the driver's window, steering one-handed. The throttle roared, dust flying around the wheels. Nate lay slumped at Kara's feet, unable to stand. This is it, she thought.

Something moved beside her, a shape striding through the flames. Strong hands pushed her aside, taking the place she'd been moments before. Lynx looked up, eyes widening in horror.

Dash held up a hand as the car sped closer, the engine screaming. Then at the last second Lynx jerked aside, twisting the wheel as the car rolled, smashing into the pyre, scattering blazing planks across the arena. Kara shielded her eyes as sparks rose, smoke billowing around

173

them. Dash turned to her. His eyes were bright.

"I couldn't let them hurt you," he said. "I just couldn't."

Kara looked up at him, struggling to focus. "Your brother's going to be mad," she managed, then the heat overcame her and she stumbled to her knees.

On Dash's orders they were taken to the medical truck where a military doctor with an ash-grey face and kind eyes inspected Kara's injuries and pronounced her essentially indestructible. But Nate's burns were more serious and the doctor suggested he spend the night under observation.

"I'll give him something to help him sleep," he said, taking Nate's arm and pushing a needle into it, ignoring the boy's feeble protests. Almost immediately Nate's eyes began to droop and Kara helped him to a small cot, resting his head on his bundled jacket.

He looked up at her, his eyes blurry and unfocused. "You saved my life," he said. "Again."

Kara shook her head. "Dash saved both of us. He stood up to his brothers."

She couldn't begin to guess what the consequences of Dash's defiance might be. Should she go to him? No, it was best to let the dust settle. Sleep on it and figure things out tomorrow.

Outside the medical truck the Wildcats were waiting, perched on a bench while the doctor inspected their cuts and bruises. They glared resentfully as Kara emerged. Lynx jumped up, blocking her way.

"Where d'you think you're going?"

Kara gestured to the yellow bus. "I'm still your prisoner, aren't I? I thought I'd lock myself in and go to sleep."

Lynx grunted suspiciously but stepped aside. "To be honest, I don't know what you are any more. One of them orders me to kill you, another one saves your life."

Kara smiled. "That must be confusing. Well, I'm too tired to escape so you may as well relax."

She staggered to the bus, pushing inside and shoving the door shut behind her. "Honestly," she muttered to herself. "What a day."

"Oh, it's not over yet," said a voice, and Kara stood bolt upright.

There was a shape at the back of the bus, someone hunched in the shadows. She peered closer in the fading light. "Show yourself," she demanded. "I'm not in the mood for games."

The figure lifted its head and Kara felt a shiver run through her. Hands reached up and she heard the soft rustle of cloth. A red glow pierced the darkness and tiny cogs ground softly.

"You saw me today," Redeye said, leaning forward into a shaft of clear moonlight. "Didn't you? I could feel it. For a moment something … stopped."

Kara could hardly breathe. It was as though an old, bad dream had broken through into the waking world. Redeye had been John Cortez's security chief; he had led the team that bombed the Wall around London. He had an artificial eye embedded in his skull, but it had never worked properly. Then, during the battle, he had lost his good eye too, blinding him completely.

"I saw you," Kara admitted. "But I didn't believe it. We're in the middle of nowhere, Redeye. What are you doing here?"

He smiled ruefully. "The same as you. Following this rabble. Waiting for a chance to stop them in their tracks, before they can reach Frisco. And I think I may have found it."

Kara approached him, trying to keep her hands from shaking. The left side of Redeye's face was just as she remembered it, the crimson glow making his white skin look even whiter. But the other side was a tortured ruin, the flesh twisted like melted plastic. He tried to smile but only half of his mouth could manage it.

"I wanted to talk to you, back at the radar station," he said. "But I didn't know how you'd react."

"That was you?" Kara asked, remembering the dark figure who had darted away from them down in the tunnels.

"Of course," Redeye said. "Joe told you about my connection to that place, right?"

Kara coughed awkwardly. "He, um, must've forgot. There's been a lot going on."

"Great," Redeye said bitterly. "I tell him my life story and he just forgets it. Well, that was where they did the surgery on my eye when I was a kid. I was a lab rat for the scientists who lived there. The new eye was supposed to fuse with my brain stem, let me see for miles and pick up heat signatures. It didn't, of course. But they were there too, this Five that everyone's so crazy about. I haven't seen their faces but I know it's them – five identical guys who spend every minute together and finish each other's sentences."

"That's them," Kara said. "They're clones."

Redeye nodded. "I figured as much, afterwards. They were only teenagers when I knew them, but they assisted in the operation."

"But why go back?" Kara asked. "If they did such bad things to you?"

"I was desperate," Redeye said. "I'm blind, Kara. You don't know what it's like. I knew it was a long shot, but

I thought maybe the scientists would've have figured out by now why the eye didn't work and be able to fix it. But there was just that old man left, and he's no use to anyone. He showed me their records, their logs, but of course I couldn't read them. Then you all showed up, and it felt like … fate."

"So you just tagged along? Hasn't anyone wondered where the pale blind guy came from?"

Redeye waved a hand. "They're soldiers – if you do what they tell you, they don't ask questions. I may not be able to see but I can scrub a shirt and polish a truck. Obviously they don't know my real intention, which is to stop The Five before it's too late. And all I need is your help."

Kara sighed. "How did I know you were going to say that?"

"Just hear me out," Redeye said. "I've got a plan – it's a good one. But first you have to understand something. The Five, they're not like regular people."

Kara laughed. "I had noticed."

"No, I don't just mean the clone thing," Redeye said. "Though that's weird enough. Let me tell you about something that happened back then, in the bunker. After those monsters took out my eye I was in pain, I was scared, I was just a kid. It was The Five's job to watch

178

over me, take my blood, see how I was responding to the transplant. But there was one in particular – he really seemed to enjoy it. He liked seeing me hurt."

Kara shuddered. She knew which of them he was referring to.

"Then one day I got the drop on him," Redeye continued. "They were all in my cell, asking questions and writing down the answers – how was the pain, could I see anything, how many fingers were they holding up. They wanted me to, you know … to *go*, in a glass jug. I acted like I was going to, then I grabbed the jug, smashed it and took the biggest shard. Slashed my fingers but I didn't care. I got hold of the one who was mean to me and I jabbed at him, cut his head open, just here."

He gestured to his eyebrow and Kara nodded. "He's still got the scar."

Redeye smiled. "Good. Anyway, I had my arm around his throat and I put the shard to his neck. I said if they didn't let me go I'd kill him. I looked up at the others and what I saw in their eyes, it was … *absolute fear.* Total panic. Like what was happening was completely beyond their ability to cope with."

"So what happened?" Kara asked. "How did they stop you?"

Redeye waved a hand. "Oh, one of the scientists snuck

up and stuck me with a needle. But that look in their eyes never left me, and years later I understood why. Have you ever seen someone lose part of their body, Kara? I have. It was in the Kuala shipyards, this guy was hauling freight when a cable got loose and snip! Took his foot right off. But the look in his eyes, it was the same one those clones had. The exact same fear."

"Of course they were scared," Kara said. "You were threatening their brother."

"Not just their brother," Redeye said. "I was threatening *them*. That's what I realised. They're not just brothers, they're closer than that. They're *one person*, Kara. One person, but split into five bodies."

Kara felt her mind roll over. Scar had said something similar, hadn't he? *We're many*, he'd said. *But we are also one.*

"Each is part of the whole," she realised out loud, as things began to add up in her mind – the way the clones spoke, their almost telepathic connection, Dash's reluctance to turn against the others. It would be like someone turning against himself.

"It's freakish," Redeye said. "But you see what I'm getting at, right? All we need to do is cut off one part, and the rest won't be able to function."

Kara flinched. "By cut off, you mean kill. Don't you?"

Redeye held up a hand. "I get it, you're not a killer,

180

blah blah blah. But you don't have to be. One of them saved your life, he trusts you. All you need to do is get him away from the others, somewhere quiet where I can—"

"No!" Kara cried out, taking a step back. "That's… How could you? And you don't even know it would work – you might just make the rest of them angrier."

"So we let Frisco burn?" Redeye spat. "We let them attack the Mariners?"

"What's this *we*?" Kara demanded. "There is no *we*, Redeye. *You* tried to take over the Shanties. *You* planted a bomb that killed thousands. We're not friends, we're not allies, we're not anything. And besides, Joe's already on his way. He'll warn your people."

Redeye snorted. "One scared kid in a crackpot flying machine? You'll forgive me if I don't love those odds. He's probably lying somewhere in the desert right now while the vultures pick his bones."

The rage welled up and Kara almost swung at him, then she remembered he was blind.

"Here's what I'll do," she said through gritted teeth. "I'll agree not to tell anyone I saw you. I'll let you leave, right this second. And in return you will never, *ever* speak to me again."

14
The Junk Maze

Joe's journey came to an abrupt end just after dawn on the second day.

He'd spent the night on the roof of a high, deserted building, the wind howling through the struts of the plane as he huddled in the cockpit. On waking he'd filled the fuel tanks and started the engine, trying to ignore the hunger in his belly and the weakness in his bones. Now he was coasting west with the sun on his shoulders, sure that today he would reach the Mariners.

Hearing a clamour, he looked down through the mesh floor. In the shadows of a shattered shopping mall he could make out a large, disorderly dog pack streaming through the parking lot and out into an empty riverbed. They followed him on the ground, snapping and barking and howling at him to come down and be eaten. But after a while the din faded, the dogs falling back as the flying machine rose over a stony ridge and a new vista opened up.

At first Joe thought the land ahead was dark because it was still in shadow; the sun hadn't yet risen over the ridge behind him. But gradually he realised that the ground itself was black, stained with a filth that seemed to have soaked into the very earth. Everywhere he looked he saw piles of refuse, heaps of metal and plastic, stacks of rusted vehicles and appliances. The junkyard stretched ahead and to either side, a sprawling metropolis of man-made waste. The smell was atrocious.

Then he saw a flash of colour and almost burst out laughing. A face beamed up at him from the rubble, thirty feet high and made from slabs of bright green plastic. It had long metallic antennae and shiny steel eyes, and beneath it on the ground some words had been written in silver paint: TAKE ME TO YOUR LEADER. Beyond it he saw another image, painted piecemeal on planks of wood – a man with eight arms and six legs, standing in a circle. There were other slogans, too: a sign made from painted stones read, WE WILL ROCK YOU; while elsewhere hundreds of electrical cables had been twisted into a bolt of lightning and the words, POWER TO THE PEOPLE!

Joe pulled on the control bar and the plane lifted, more pictures and slogans revealing themselves with every foot of altitude. He saw faces and trees and religious symbols, a huge red soup tin made from smaller red soup tins. In the centre of the junkyard was an expanse of whitewashed stone several hundred feet wide, with the words IT'S A SAD AND BEAUTIFUL WORLD painted on it in looping purple script. Joe considered this, and thought it might be the truest thing he'd ever read.

Then, gradually, two very different sounds began to make themselves known to him. From behind, a good distance away but still approaching, he could hear the ferocious barking of the dogs. And much closer, and growing louder, a groan was emanating from the engine.

Joe twisted, looking back. Smoke was rising, just a wisp at first, but very black. Then the motor coughed and the smoke thickened, billowing from a ventilator in the side. There was a wave of heat and he just had time to cover his face before the engine exploded, side-panels tearing loose in a burst of blue chemical fire.

The propeller spun to a stop and silence fell, broken only by the faint yapping of the dogs. The plane's nose tilted steadily downward, gliding on a current of air as gravity took hold. Joe gritted his teeth as the ground rushed up to meet him and he heard a bone-shattering crunch as one of the wings slammed into a leaning tower of rubbish, sending them into a wild spin. He gripped the seat, curling up tight as he was pulled in every direction at once.

The spiralling plane struck a stack of metal sheets, the wheels and both wings shearing clean off before the body finally bellyflopped into a mountain of refuse and came to rest. Head spinning, Joe checked himself. His hands were trembling and there was a cut on his cheek, but the chain between his cuffs had snapped on impact, which was actually pretty helpful. He climbed out of the wreck, staggering a little. All in all, it could've been worse.

Then he heard barking, and realised it was. Piles of junk rose all around him: sheets of steel and synthetics, landslides of broken glass, sacks spilling rotted paper and mulchy filth. And over the peak of a plastic mountain came the dog pack, their teeth bared and glistening.

Joe stumbled back, his limbs weak. But he had no choice – he began to run, leaving the broken plane behind, just more wreckage for the pile. The air was hot and foul but there seemed to be pathways through the rubbish, so he followed them, skirting a tangle of rusty bicycles, hopping over a flyblown puddle of greyish slime and darting between an oily heap of boat parts and a stack of magazines bound with rope.

The barking grew louder and, glancing back, Joe could see the lead dog barely thirty feet behind and closing. Its muzzle was brown and its teeth were sharp, but beneath its patchy fur he could see ribs poking through. They're starving, he thought. Just like me.

Some of the dogs were small, stumpy legs scurrying madly as they yapped and yammered. Others were as big as Joe – sandy creatures with narrow snouts and an untamed look in their eyes. He splashed through a swamp of glittering oil, the lead animal's teeth snapping at his ankles. A stack of wooden furniture loomed ahead and he grabbed the leg of a chair, yanking as hard as he could. The heap toppled, wardrobes and tables crashing and splintering. The dogs scattered; a few weren't fast enough and were pinned in the landslide.

But the rest recovered and rejoined the chase, bounding over fallen furnishings as Joe blundered on, his muscles aching, his breath coming in short, desperate gasps. There had to be someone here, someone who had made all those signs and pictures. It was just a case of finding them before the dogs caught him, before they ran him down and ripped him to—

He skidded to a stop. Ahead of him was a hole, a circular well too wide to leap over. Rubble heaps sloped down on all sides – he could try to clamber over them but

186

he didn't fancy his chances. A stench rose from the hole and the air was hazy.

He turned to see the lead dog slowing, watching warily as it padded closer. Joe could almost read its thoughts – the boy tricked us before, he might do it again. But it wouldn't be long before they realised he was helpless. Wind whistled through the rubbish piles, and Joe felt a deep sadness wash over him. What a lonely place to die.

Then he heard something behind him, a human voice, echoing as though— Yes. He turned to the edge of the hole, peering down. There was movement in the depths and he cupped his hands around his mouth. "Hello?" he shouted. "I need help!"

With a growl the lead dog sprang. Joe dodged feebly as it bore down on him, teeth flashing. Luckily he was a small target; the creature missed by a whisker, skidding to earth and turning. The others drew in but the leader barked at them to stay back – Joe belonged to *him*. The dog crouched, preparing to leap, and Joe heard a peculiar fizzing noise.

Something bright and sparkling rose from the hole, twisting into the air. The dog raised its snout, perplexed, and Joe watched as the little spark reached the top of its arc and began to descend. Then there was a terrific bang and the spark burst apart, emitting a flash of white light and a spiral of smaller, brighter sparks, all green and gold.

The dogs drew back, ears flat. Another spark rose and they whined, retreating. When it burst with a pop they turned tail, streaming through the rubbish, the lead dog bringing up the rear. It glanced resentfully back at Joe, eyes narrowed. Then it was gone.

"Works every time."

The deep voice echoed up from the hole and Joe saw a large figure scaling the inside of the pit, using shelves of refuse to clamber up into the daylight. She was clad from head to toe in rustling black plastic, climbing hand over muscled hand, and Joe wondered weakly if he hadn't stumbled from one calamity into another.

The stranger rose, throwing Joe into shadow. She took a step towards him and the ground shook; looking down he saw a solid metal foot sinking into the mud. The stranger peeled back a protective mask to reveal dark eyes and an unsmiling face covered with circling black tattoos.

"Don't hurt me," Joe managed, but his head was starting to spin. "Please, I need to…"

Then the world seemed to tip and he sat down with a bump, all the strength gone out of him.

Afterwards he could recall only fragments of what happened next; his head was all blurry and his body felt like the juice had been wrung out of it. He remembered the woman advancing on him, reaching down and lifting him in her arms. He remembered light in his eyes, sunbeams glaring from sheets of glass and metal as they moved through the maze of junk. And he remembered the relief of shade, as the stranger placed him down and reached for a bottle, pressing it to his lips.

Sticky-sweet liquid filled Joe's mouth and he coughed, scrambling up. The stranger stood over him, seeming to fill the entire shadowed space.

"It's only Fizzy Fango," she said. "Found a whole case last week. Drink up." She placed a hand on Joe's chest and pressed the bottle to his lips again, forcing him to swallow. Immediately he felt stronger, the sugar in the drink setting his nerves alight.

"Where am I?" he asked. "And who are you?"

The stranger put the bottle down, taking a step back. He heard floorboards creak and saw that metal foot again, gleaming dully in the slanting light.

"Made that myself," she told him. "First year here. Got a cut, got infected, had to lop the old one off. Perils of living in a junkyard."

Joe inched back, eyeing her nervously. The woman was big – broad across the shoulders and heavy with muscle. And she hadn't smiled once – that wasn't a good sign.

"Why did you bring me here?" he asked, looking around. They were in a shack with no windows and a sloping clapboard roof. He assumed the walls were wood too but he couldn't say for sure because they were plastered with pictures – pages from books and magazines, posters and billboards and advertisements. Most of them seemed to feature faces, and as he looked around Joe felt like he was in a weird sort of theatre, an audience of motionless people grinning down at him.

"Those are all my favourites," the woman said. "That's Marilyn, and there's Freddie, and this is Franklin Del Rio, the biggest star of them all."

Joe squinted. "But who are they?"

The woman shook her head. "Who *were* they, that's the question. They were great, but now they're gone. Here, listen to this. I only just dug it up and I can't get enough of it."

She reached for a small plastic device and ran her finger over it, her tattooed face lit by a beam of artificial light. Then she hit a button and Joe jumped in surprise as music blasted through the shack, a jagged, rhythmic sound with wailing voices over the top.

The woman closed her eyes and swayed, her face relaxing as she listened. Joe glanced past her to the half-open door, sunlight slanting through. If he ran he might make it, be gone before she opened her eyes. But then what? This place was a maze and he had no idea how to navigate it.

"Do you like it?" the woman asked loudly. "It's good, right? Powerful."

Joe nodded. "It's ... interesting," he managed.

"They're called Cyclical Puppy," she told him. "This was recorded in 2062, right before the second big crash. You know, people today think of Tech-Age folks as either gods or idiots – they invented computers and went to the moon but at the same time they ruined the world for everyone who came after. But it's so much more complicated than that. If you watch their movies and hear their music you find out that most of them dreamed of a very different future than this one, and they kept on creating, despite all the wars and the famines and everything else."

The song faded and Joe stared up at her, wondering what was going on. Had she brought him here to eat him, or lecture him, or what?

"And that's what you do?" he asked politely. "Dig up stuff from the olden days?"

The woman shrugged. "It passes the time. If you dig far enough, you can find artefacts going back hundreds of years, and so much of it is just ... beautiful. I guess a lot of it just got forgotten about over the years, and the world's sadder for it."

"It's a sad and beautiful world," Joe said, remembering the message he'd seen from above. "You made those signs, didn't you? The pictures and the words."

The woman blushed. "I made them. That one's from an old movie. But how did you see them?"

Joe told her about the flying machine, how he'd crashed into the junk. "I'm trying to reach the Mariners," he said. "Do you know where I can find them?"

The woman's eyes darkened. "I know where they are. But you should rest – you're weak."

Joe struggled to his feet. "You can't keep me here, you know. I'm small but I can still fight."

"Hey," the woman said, taking a step back. "Who said anything about keeping you here?"

"Well, you're a lot bigger than me," Joe said. "And you don't exactly live in a normal sort of place. I know there's bandits round here, and cannibals. And your tattoos and your leg are quite scary."

The woman stared at him, then her face cracked and for the first time she smiled. She put out a hand. "I'm sorry, I don't get a lot of visitors. It's been months since I had an actual conversation and I've obviously forgotten how. My name's Lenny and I'm not a bandit or a cannibal, I promise."

Joe hesitated, then he reached up and shook. "I'm Joe," he said. "I'm pleased to meet you. But I meant it before – I really, really have to get to the Mariners as soon as possible."

The woman shrugged. "All right then," she said. "Have another drink and let's go."

They climbed a steep rise between heaps of corrugated metal and the rusted shells of cars, Lenny's metal leg thumping the ground as they walked. The going was sometimes hard, sometimes swampy, and Joe wondered how far down the rubbish went and what the valley had looked like before people started using it as a junkyard. Occasionally they saw other figures in the labyrinth, shadowy forms darting beneath heaps of scrap or watching them from a distance. But no one came near or spoke to them, and Joe was glad of Lenny's solid presence at his side.

As they walked he told her about the Shanties, which she'd heard of but never seen, and about The Five, who for Lenny were just a vague rumour.

"I'm sorry I didn't trust you," Joe said. "But where I come from most folks are out for themselves. People only help each other if there's something in it for them."

Lenny laughed. "Well, maybe there is something in it

for me – did you think of that? If I help you get where you need to go, it makes me feel better about myself. I remember that even though I live in a heap of junk I'm still a decent person. So by helping you, I'm still helping me."

Joe smiled at her. "That's a nice way of looking at it."

They stopped at the top of the slope to catch their breath and behind them he saw the huge pictures and messages spread out under the fading sky.

"Is that why you make those?" he asked. "Because they make you feel better about things?"

Lenny shrugged. "I think I just wanted to bring some beauty back into the world. It's not much, but it's the best I can do. Now look, over there."

Joe followed her finger. Ahead of them the junk kept going, down into a rocky ravine then up another steep slope. But on its peak, running north to south, a solid metal structure rose from the rubbish. "That fence marks the Mariner border," Lenny said. "And we're right on time – they usually make a drop around sunset."

"What do you mean, a drop?" Joe asked. "You mean the Mariners leave their junk here too?"

Lenny nodded. "Every day, like clockwork. Why are you so surprised?"

"I don't know," Joe said. "I just thought they were different."

They scrambled down into the gully then up the other side, climbing over heaps of fresh trash: food waste, rusted metal and broken nets. Above them the fence rose, twenty feet high and made from plates of grey steel. "It's not that tall," Joe said as they approached. "Not compared to the Wall at home. They can't be very serious about keeping people out."

"I think it's more of a statement," Lenny told him. "This is ours, so stay away."

There was a sudden electric whine and Joe heard cogs grinding. A section of the fence began to rise, sliding up like a panel. Lenny tugged him aside as something came tumbling through the gap – more refuse, some of it bagged but most just rolling loose. He saw old clothes and smashed glass and pieces of a motor, and there was a strong stench of rotten fish.

Then the rubbish slide abated and Joe peered through. Beyond the fence he could see a cluttered yard and a yellow vehicle, squat and blocky with a steel plate fixed to the front. The plate dropped down and the vehicle advanced, pushing another heap of refuse through the gap. There were two figures inside: a red-faced man at the wheel and a girl in uniform at his side. Joe waved but they didn't spot him; the girl was engrossed in a book and the man was too intent on his work. But as the vehicle retreated again Joe stepped out, waving. The man saw him and rolled his eyes, nudging the girl.

"No junk-roaches today," he said, sticking his head out of the window. "The refugee centre's about sixty miles that way." And he jerked a thumb towards the south.

"I'm not a refugee," Joe shouted back. "I've come to warn you."

The junkman frowned. "About what, poor life choices?"

"Not just you, all the Mariners," Joe said. "There's an army coming to wipe you out."

The junkman laughed. "An army? Of what, grimy little trash-pickers like you?"

"Of men," Joe said. "In big trucks. Look, I was on the *Neptune*. We were attacked by pirates and—"

"The *Neptune*? I suppose you're best friends with John Cortez too?"

"No," Joe snapped. "I was one of the ones who stopped him."

The junkman snorted. "You're creative, I'll give you that. But now you need to back up before you end up under the tracks of my 'dozer." He flicked a switch and the engine started up again.

Joe looked back at Lenny. "They won't listen. They think I'm just some poor scavenger kid."

"You are some poor scavenger kid," she said. "But

that's nothing to be ashamed of. Now get out there and tell 'em."

Joe looked at the dozer as it rumbled forward, the trash piling up against the blade. Then he took a deep breath and stepped directly in its path. The junkman's eyes widened as the rubbish rolled higher, looming over Joe, ready to topple down and swamp him. Joe braced himself, but at the last minute the girl reached over and switched off the engine.

"Look, we really can't help you," she said. "He's just a junkman and I'm just his escort, and neither of us has the authority to allow you across the border. So get lost, before you force me to do something I'll regret." She placed a hand on the pistol at her waist.

Joe faced her and felt a surge of anger. "I came a long way," he said bitterly. "I got attacked by pirates and stole a plane and ran from some dogs, and I didn't do it all just to be … to be … *insulted*. I heard the Mariners were decent people, at least most of them. Nate told us John Cortez was a bad example, that most of you were good, and I believed h—"

"Wait, back up," the girl said. "You say you were on the *Neptune* with a kid called Nate? What did he look like?"

"About this tall," Joe told her. "Sort of roundish, though not as much as he used to be. His Aunt Sedna's on the Council, but he's back in the desert with this army I told you about."

"There was a boy called Nate a couple of years below me at Junior Academy," the girl said, turning excitedly to the driver. "We used to bunk off and draw Aquaboy comics together. But just last week I read a report that he'd been lost at sea, after…"

She looked at Joe and her eyes were filled with amazement.

"After a pirate attack. Kid, you'd better start talking."

15

The Calm

Shapes rose from the rolling dunes, statues and towers and fountains, all smoothed by time and the ever-shifting sand. Some were several stories high, ancient buildings with shattered glass in the windows and drifts piling against their crumbling walls. A sign read HOTEL PARADISE WEDDINGS PERFORMED 24/7, and although Kara understood most of the words, they didn't seem to make sense put together like that. Tattered curtains lifted in the breeze and she caught a glimpse of one of the rooms within – a red carpet, a mouldering bed, flowers on the walls, all drowning in waves and ripples and streams and rivers of drifting, ceaseless, all-consuming sand.

But the desert wasn't the only intruder in this dead place. The Five's army had descended that afternoon, hurtling along the concrete highway that pierced the city like the shaft of an arrow. Now the trucks stood in smoking rows between the buildings, ticking like insects as their engines cooled. It was the last gathering before they reached Mariner country. The last chance to make a difference.

Kara stood in the doorway of the school bus, watching as a crowd began to form, soldiers leaving their vehicles and making their way down the sandy street. She'd barely slept last night, going over and over what Redeye had told her. It all made so much sense, this idea that The Five were one person, their individual personalities just fragments of the whole. She wondered how they'd come to be that way – was it part of their parents' plan? Or was it inevitable?

Grey was their centre, she knew, their voice of reason. Scar was their spite, their cruelty, their anger. Knuckles was their humour, and Boxer their aggression. And Dash was their kindness, their decency. But now he had gone against his brothers, he had saved Kara's life. Which meant that this person – this divided individual that called itself The Five – was capable of changing its mind.

Hearing a groan, she turned back. Nate lay unconscious on the bus's front bench, his face red with blisters. The doctor had brought him back that morning along with a pack of sleeping syringes, instructing Kara to use them if the boy was in a lot of pain.

"Just a little, at first," he'd cautioned. "It's strong stuff."

There was no sign of Lynx, but Kara wasn't surprised. Their jailer had barely spoken on the drive down here, not even bothering to lock Kara's cuffs. Perhaps Lynx figured it was too late for Kara to affect anything now. Perhaps it was.

She sat on the bench beside Nate, touching him gently on the cheek. "Wake up."

The boy's eyes fluttered and he smiled blearily. "I was having such a good dream," he said. "Me and you and Joe were in Frisco, we were safe. We went swimming and Cane was there. She seemed terribly sad about something. But then Joe showed us all how to turn ourselves into penguins by sticking our thumbs in our mouths and blowing, and that cheered her up."

"I have to go out," Kara said quickly, before he could keep rambling. "Just for a little while."

Nate's face darkened. "Go where? What are you going to do?"

Kara bit her lip. "I need to talk to Dash. And to his brothers, if they'll listen."

Nate tried to rise. "No, Kara, that's not a good idea. They'll—"

"The attack is tomorrow," she said bluntly. "If I don't

act now, it'll be too late."

Nate started to protest then he stopped himself, shaking his head. "I should know better by now, shouldn't I? I nearly got us all killed, twice. Meanwhile you got The Five to trust you and one of them ended up saving us. You're amazing, Kara. Whatever you need to do, you should do it."

Kara blushed, shaking her head, but before she could speak Nate had reached up, gripping her shoulder with a blistered hand and pulling her down towards him. Kara felt her balance go as her face smacked into his, their lips bumping together, their foreheads colliding with a clunk. Nate whimpered in pain and Kara pulled back, looking at him in astonishment.

"What are you *doing*?" she asked.

Nate blushed, his red face turning even redder. "I'm sorry, I just… Maybe it's that stuff the doctor gave me."

Kara could feel her pulse throbbing where their heads had smacked together; she knew she'd have a bruise. "Honestly," she said. "I think we've got enough to worry about, don't you?"

She'd meant it as a joke, something to lighten the painfully awkward mood. But looking into Nate's eyes she could see how much it hurt.

"I'm sorry," he muttered again. "I only meant…"

"It's OK," Kara told him. "Forget it. Try and sleep."

"But…" Nate protested as Kara pushed him down.

"I mean it. I really have to go."

Avoiding his gaze, she backed down the steps and into the sandswept street. The sun was sinking, painting the horizon in bronze and blue. At the end of the palm-fringed boulevard The Five's stage truck stood ready, searchlights sweeping the sky. Beyond it Kara could make out the two huge vehicles the Arizona Brigade had brought with them – their contents remained a mystery, and she'd never seen anyone going in or out. But she didn't have time to worry about it now.

She followed the flow of people, feeling that awful, wrongheaded kiss still on her lips. Had it been a surprise? Or had she been expecting this – bracing for it almost? Her whole life she'd been so busy finding food and shelter for herself and Joe that she'd never even had time for friends, let alone … anything else. It just seemed like more trouble than it was worth – she could look after herself and she could just about manage to keep an eye on Joe, but anyone else would be a burden. She knew that was a tough way of looking at it but it also happened to be true.

Soldiers pressed in around her, just like that night in the showground eight days and half a lifetime ago. But there was a tension in the air that hadn't been there

203

before, a sense of urgency in every muttered word, every upturned eye. Music pulsated, growing in volume until it hammered on Kara's ears. A flock of crows spiralled into the air as the wall of a building collapsed into the sand.

Then the side of the stage-truck dropped and white beams blazed out, brighter than the setting sun. Soldiers cheered, the sound rolling back in waves. The Five took the stage, their suits gleaming, their teeth polished, not a hair out of place.

"It is *time*," Scar began, the last word falling like a stone.

"Time to step up," Grey continued.

"Time to fight back." That was Knuckles.

"Time to fight hard." Boxer braced his fists.

"Time to fight for everything you b——" Something caught in Dash's throat and he coughed, punching his chest. "Believe in."

Scar shot him a look, his eyes flashing.

"Our weather experts say there's a storm coming," Grey went on.

"You can feel the wind rising," Knuckles agreed, licking a finger and holding it in the air.

"We think it's a sign," Boxer said.

"A signal from the heavens," Dash added, glancing upward.

"That our crusade is justified," Scar said. "That our

mission is right and true."

He took the lead, the others lining up on either side.

"From here the DustRoad turns north."

"Avoiding the lands that the Mariners stole."

"But we will not turn aside."

"We will go west, towards our destiny."

"Tomorrow we begin to unite this troubled nation."

"Tomorrow we take back the power and the dignity they stole from us."

"The right to live our own lives."

"To make our own laws."

"To build our own nation in peace and prosperity!"

It didn't make complete sense, but Kara knew it didn't have to. The speech was designed simply to fire up the crowd, get them ready for the battle to come. She found herself strangely unmoved – it was such a bare-faced attempt to manipulate the audience that she was able to stand apart from it, unpicking each phrase in her head. The crowd was rapt, but to her it was just a long, rambling lie.

It didn't help that Dash's attention kept wandering – at one point he trod on Boxer's foot, at another he seemed to forget his line entirely, stuttering until Grey picked up the slack. Kara watched, and hope rose in her heart. Dash didn't just seem distracted, he seemed downright unsure of what he was saying. Almost as if he didn't believe in it any more.

As the show reached its crescendo the clones strode to the front, the lights from below throwing their identical features into crisp relief. "Of course," Scar said, gazing out at the convoy. "None of this would be possible without one person."

"One incredible person," Boxer nodded.

"Someone who has given everything," said Grey.

"Everything they own," Dash added.

"Everything they *are*," Knuckles insisted.

"To make this world a better place," Scar finished.

They looked at one another and nodded theatrically, then they turned and pointed at the audience. "That person is you."

"You answered the call."

"You gave, and you gave."

"You asked for nothing in return."

"But that's too bad." Grey gave a cockeyed grin. "Because we're going to give it to you anyway."

There was a screech of tyres and Kara saw three vehicles skidding to a halt in front of the stage. The Wildcats jumped out, grinning at the crowd and high-fiving each other. Strapped to the roofs of their cars Kara could see three motionless shapes – slumped forms almost as large as the cars themselves. Then someone shouted, "Step back!" and a bonfire erupted, flames rising towards the sky. In the flickering light Kara saw glassy eyes and lolling tongues, and realised what the Wildcats had brought — three dead cows strapped to the roofs of their cars.

Leo cut a rope and one of the animals crashed down in the dust. Soldiers came flocking from every direction, wielding axes and cleavers and even swords. There was a chorus of thuds and squelches, and Kara looked away in disgust.

"So we've got meat," The Five said. "And of course we've got beer."

They gestured to a white van, the rear doors flying open to reveal stacks of crates.

"Tonight, we celebrate."

"Because tomorrow, we fight!"

This time the applause was deafening, the city shaking with the force of it. The soldiers swarmed forward, eager to get into the refreshments. The Five were leaving the stage, retreating down the metal steps at the rear of the truck. Everyone was distracted, even the security guards — Kara saw one of them wading into the mob, snatching a bottle from a smaller man's hand and downing it.

So she shoved back, forcing through the crowd. No

one tried to stop her as she reached the stage truck and slipped underneath, scrambling between the tyres into the enclosure beyond. The wind had picked up and the air was full of blowing sand, but through the murk she could see a pair of figures moving away from her – two of The Five striding towards the train car. But where were the rest?

Hearing voices, she ducked behind a trailer.

"What *was* that?" one of the clones barked furiously. "What's happening to you?"

"I'm sorry," another spluttered, and Kara knew it was Dash. "I'm just tired. Things have been so crazy."

"It's that girl," a third voice sneered. "Don't deny it."

Kara peered around the trailer. They were a short distance away, Dash backed against the stage truck with Boxer's hand around his throat. Scar stood to the side, spittle flying from his lips.

"She's *nothing*," he was saying, raising his voice above the wind. "A treacherous child who has been working against us from the start. Why does she mean so much to you?"

"Because she's different," Dash blurted. "She listens to me. Not to The Five, to *me*."

Scar shook his head. "That's the most pathetic thing I've ever heard. You *are* us. We *are* you. And you'd better not mess things up tomorrow. This is everything we've worked for and I won't let you—"

"Don't move," a voice said. "Stay right where you are."

Kara saw a figure emerging from the clouds of sand, his ragged coat flapping. She saw a red flicker and a raised pistol. "I mean it," Redeye ordered, the gun trembling in his hand. "I'll shoot." He looked exhausted and desperate, like he knew this wasn't going to work.

"Who are you?" Scar demanded, turning to face him. "What do you want?"

Redeye adjusted his aim. "You know who I am, clone. And you know what you did to me."

"Redeye," Kara said, stepping from her hiding place. "I told you. This isn't the way."

The blind man turned instinctively towards her, keeping his pistol trained on Scar. All around them the wind was rising, the sand lashing in strengthening gusts.

"Redeye?" Scar asked in amazement. "The one who planted the bomb? Well, this is an honour."

"We've met before," Redeye said. "Don't you remember? You tortured me. You helped those scientists take out my eye." He gestured to his face and a cold smile lit up Scar's features.

"Incredible," he said. "We thought you died in the desert. You were such a weak little thing."

"I was a child!" Redeye screamed, his hands shaking. "I was in pain and you laughed at me. I gave you something to remember me, though, didn't I? And now I'm going to finish what I started."

He stepped forward, his finger on the trigger. Without thinking, Kara sprang.

She crossed the space between them in two strides, hearing the gun go off as she slammed into Redeye's side. She heard a cry of pain then they hit the ground together, rolling and tumbling. She grabbed Redeye's arm and slammed it into the ground, forcing him to let go of the gun. Boxer stepped forward, kicking it away.

Behind him Scar stood clutching his face, blood leaking between his fingers. He removed his hand and Kara saw a deep groove in the skin just above his ear. Dash stood behind him, looking in astonishment at a bullet hole in the truck tyre, air whistling through it.

Kara climbed to her feet but Redeye stayed where he was, prone on the dusty tarmac. "Why did you do that?" he demanded in disbelief. "It was our chance!"

"You know me," Kara said. "I don't like killing."

"But we're on the same side this time," Redeye protested. "Neptune's beard, you're impossible."

Kara helped him up. "If it makes you feel any better, you've definitely given him another scar."

Footsteps sounded as Grey and Knuckles came running from the gloom. "What happened?" Grey demanded. "We heard a shot."

"He happened," Scar said, gesturing at Redeye.

"He wanted to kill us," Boxer added.

"But Kara stepped in," Dash said, looking at her proudly.

Boxer took hold of Redeye, yanking his arms behind his back. Scar strode forward but Kara stepped between them. "Don't hurt him," she said.

Scar sneered through the blood on his face. "Give me one reason why not."

"Because I'm asking you," Kara replied.

Grey crossed his arms, looking searchingly at her. "Why did you stop him?" he asked. "With one of us dead we'd have had to call off the attack. I thought that's what you wanted."

"Not like this," Kara said. "In fact, I came here to try and reason with you. Or at least with Dash."

Grey frowned. "Dash? Who is Dash?"

Kara flushed. "He is," she said, pointing at his brother. "We, um … we gave you all names. Joe and Nate and me. It's because of his birthmark, you know, dot dash."

Dash stared at her in astonishment, then he smiled. "Dash. I like it."

"And what did you call me?" Knuckles asked. "Devilishly Handsome?"

Boxer barked a laugh, but Grey shook his head. "We do not need names, Kara. We're The Five. We are one."

"But you're not," she insisted. "You act like it, but deep down you're all a little bit different. Dash saved me, doesn't that prove it?"

"Minor variations," Grey said. "Tiny differences in character, no more important than the colour of my hair or the mark on my brother's wrist."

To her surprise, Kara could see uncertainty in his eyes. This whole idea worries him, she realised. The thought that they could be in any way different.

"So you came to reason with us," Dash put in. "With me. What were you going to say?"

"I was going to say that you don't have to do this," Kara told him. "That very first night you said you weren't evil – now here's your chance to prove it. I know the Mariners haven't done enough to help people out here, but attacking them isn't the answer. It'll only make things worse."

Scar snorted but Grey regarded Kara, eyes shining in the gloom. "So what is the answer, in your opinion?"

"Talk to them," Kara said. "Tell the Mariners why you're angry. If you're reasonable they will be too, I know

212

it. They're not who you think they are. Most of them, anyway."

"It's been tried before," Knuckles said. "Trade deals and treaties. The Mariners wouldn't listen."

"And who was doing the talking?" Kara asked. "Some war chief? Some state sheriff trying to get an advantage over his rivals? Things are different now – the states are united. They can't ignore that."

"But this army was raised for a single purpose," Scar argued. "To destroy the Mariners. That's what brought these people together."

"No, you did," Kara said. "Those soldiers worship you. If you tell them the plan's changed, they'll go along with it."

"We've never run from a fight before," Boxer growled. "And we're not going to start now."

"You shouldn't," Redeye smirked. "I'll enjoy watching my people thrash you."

"We've always done what we had to do," Dash said, ignoring him. "We were tough when we needed to be. But Kara's right, we're not evil. It's always been about survival and doing what we can for the people out here. If there's a better way, why not take it?"

Knuckles nodded thoughtfully, but Scar just sneered. "Brothers, be serious. Why did we come all this way if we're just going to act like cowards?"

"Negotiation isn't cowardice," Dash insisted. "It's just being practical."

"Listen," Grey said, turning on them. "Kara might have a point. If we can achieve our aims without sacrificing lives, it could be worth attempting. We have no guarantee we'll even win this fight – yes, we have a few tricks up our sleeve, but so might they."

Scar's eyes flashed. "So you just expect us to—"

"However," Grey said firmly. "You are also correct. We risk making ourselves look weak, and there's no sense trying to negotiate anything from a position of weakness. The Mariners don't know us. They probably think we're just a band of desert raiders come to plunder their storehouses. We've given them no reason to think otherwise."

"So what are you saying?" Kara asked. "You want to send a message? I could talk to them and—"

"That won't be enough," Grey told her. "I'm sorry, but they need to know how strong we are, and what we're willing to do. The attack must proceed as planned – we've come too far to stop now."

Scar smiled smugly as Kara started to protest.

"But here's what I suggest," Grey said, holding up a hand. "Tomorrow we'll smash through their border, and we'll rip down their fence. We'll advance into their territory and we won't stop until we reach Frisco. But when we do, I say we give Kara her chance. Once they've seen what we're capable of, once they're suitably impressed, then we'll negotiate."

"But people will still die," Kara said. "You won't cross the border without a fight."

"A fight is inevitable," Grey told her, almost sympathetically. "It always was. Just as your people needed to band together against John Cortez, so ours need to unite against Frisco. But at least this way we can keep things from escalating further."

Kara eyed him doubtfully. "You have to promise me you'll talk. Promise that whatever happens, however bad the fighting gets, when you reach the city you'll negotiate."

"I promise," Grey nodded.

"So do I," Dash replied.

"And me," Knuckles added.

Boxer turned doubtfully towards Scar, who was still shaking his head. "They won't listen," he said. "They'll take advantage of any ceasefire to smash us to pieces."

"That's a risk we'll have to take," Grey told him. "Because I'm afraid you're outvoted."

"But how will we contact them?" Knuckles asked. "Once we're in range we can send a radio signal, but how will they know what frequency we're on, or that we're broadcasting at all?"

"Someone needs to tell them we'll be calling," Kara said. "And I know just who to send."

16

The Battle
of Badwater

By the time Joe reached the Mariner outpost, the dawn was breaking and the sandstorm had begun to abate. Through the windscreen he could see the sky growing pale as gusts battered the little jeep.

After some debate, the junkman's escort had allowed him to pass under the border fence – Lenny wasn't allowed to come with him, but she didn't seem too heartbroken about it. "For better or worse, this junkpile is my home," she'd said. "Maybe one day you'll come back and visit."

"I'll bring my friends," Joe had promised her. "And we'll all make one of your pictures."

The security guard was called Mary Black Crow, which Joe thought was probably the coolest name ever. She'd sat him down while the junkman finished his work, listening

217

with mounting amazement as Joe told his story. He wasn't sure how much of it she'd believed, but she'd agreed to take him to meet her commanding officer, fifty miles north at a place called Camp Badwater.

Now Joe could see lights shimmering ahead through clouds of dust, the remnants of the sandstorm that had swept through overnight. Black Crow showed her credentials to a uniformed officer and he waved them towards the camp, a cluster of concrete buildings at the foot of a rocky desert slope.

"This place is pretty small," Joe said as they stepped from the jeep, the wind snatching at their clothes. "How many men do they have?"

"An entire division," Black Crow said. "That's more than two hundred soldiers."

Joe gulped. "It won't be enough."

They headed for the compound but before they could reach it, an iron door swung open and a ruddy-faced man strode out. He returned Black Crow's salute, peering at her over a bristly black moustache. "I hear you drove all night to see me," he barked. "Well, come on, private, what's the ruckus?"

Black Crow ushered Joe forward. "General Jardine, I found this boy in the junkyard near Salvation Point. He's got a story to tell you."

The General smiled indulgently, medals winking on his chest. "Does he now? Well, speak up lad."

Joe told his tale as briefly as he could, trying to explain about the clones and their army without making the whole thing sound ridiculous. When the General whipped off his cap and laughed, he knew he'd failed.

"You've had quite a journey," Jardine chuckled. "And this Five sound like a real bad bunch. But look around, this camp is heavily fortified. We deal with raider bands all the time."

Joe looked down towards the border fence, rising in the dawn light. It was much taller here, forming a defensive barricade around the outpost. It was studded with lookout towers too, all mounted with rotating energy cannons.

"But they're not just raiders," he insisted. "There's, like, thousands of them. And they have guns and massive trucks."

"But trucks are no good here," the General said, pointing past the fence to the flatlands beyond. The air was still thick with dust but through it Joe could see that the ground was a pale whitish colour, like the salt left behind after the tide goes out.

"D'you know what they call this place?" Jardine asked. "Its name is Death Valley, and even back in the Tech Age it was the hottest place on earth. Nowadays you can't even stand out there in full daylight without an aircon suit. If those trucks try to cross, their engines will overheat, their tyres will burst, their drivers will pass out from heatstroke. The battle will be won before it even starts."

Joe studied the Mariner defences and tried to be convinced. It didn't feel especially hot to him, but of course the sun had only just risen. Which sparked a thought.

"Hang on," he said. "What would happen if they crossed this death place at n—"

"Sir!"

The General turned as an officer came running towards them up the slope, his face red with exertion. He saluted, trying to catch his breath. "We've lost contact with two of our scouts," he reported. "They were on patrol in the valley and scheduled to check in a half-hour ago. We thought it might be the sandstorm kicking up interference but it's almost over now and still no word."

The General frowned, replacing his cap as he surveyed the salt flats. The sand still blew, obscuring the sun's pale glimmer. Joe squinted, sure for a moment that he'd seen something inside those churning clouds.

"Send another patrol," Jardine ordered. "Tell them to take all precautions for— Who in the heck is that?"

Following his gaze, Joe saw a figure beyond the fence,

sprinting towards the camp. The dust clouds boiled as he staggered then picked himself up, waving madly. The General unclipped a macrotelescope from his belt, training it. "Doesn't look like one of ours," he said. "Tell the men to ready a warning shot."

Joe gestured to the 'scope. "Can I see?"

Jardine handed it over and Joe squinted through, trying to pick out the hurtling figure. He twisted the focus and his mouth dropped.

"It's Nate!" he said. "Private Black Crow, it's him, it really is. Oh, tell them not to shoot him!"

Black Crow grabbed the 'scope, looking in amazement. "Joe's right," she said. "General, I know him. He's from Frisco. He's just a kid."

The General scowled. "Send someone to fetch him," he told his aide. "Have him brought here."

A panel lifted in the fence and a jeep sped out, hurtling towards Nate. But then Black Crow gave a gasp, raising the 'scope to inspect the dust cloud. "Sir, I don't think he's alone down there."

Joe shielded his eyes, trying to work out what was happening. There was something moving inside those clouds of sand, something dark and determined.

Then a strong wind blew, the dust was driven back and The Five's army was revealed.

They came sweeping across the salt plain, riding a wave of billowing sand. Windshields and wheel rims shone in the sudden sunlight, and their engines rumbled like approaching thunder.

In the centre was the stage truck, gun turrets rising from the roof. The train car followed, gleaming in the desert light, ahead of two big black lorries that Joe hadn't seen before. To either side, the smaller vehicles spread out like a bow wave, a charging mass of steel and rubber and smoke.

"Man the defences!" General Jardine screamed. "Get to your posts!"

Alarms wailed and Joe saw doors flying open all across the camp, men streaming out with rifles and radios, some still tugging on their uniforms. They swarmed down towards the fence, watching in disbelief as the army thundered closer. The lone jeep had reached Nate; a door flew open and he tumbled into the back. The jeep skidded in a desperate circle, pelting for the safety of the fence.

Atop the sentry towers the energy cannons spun and spat, blue firebolts striking just ahead of the advancing army. Fountains of white erupted, then the cannons fired again and this time they made contact. Engines exploded, oil and chem fuel catching fire in the air and raining down. The sound arrived late, the boom of the initial explosion followed by the scream of twisted metal.

"They're outgunned," Black Crow said, clutching Joe's shoulder. "Those cannons will tear them apart."

But Joe wasn't convinced. He saw the frontmost vehicles slowing, the attack line breaking as the smaller ones picked up speed, darting for the fence. One in particular broke from the pack – a tiny, reinforced assault vehicle, gaining momentum as it powered across the flat.

"They need to blast him," Joe said, pointing desperately. "They need to blast him now!"

Someone on the ground clearly had the same idea – the energy cannons swivelled, blue bolts sending up jets of sand and salt. But the vehicle swerved clear, skidding as it closed on the fence. Joe saw the door fly open, the driver flinging himself out, rolling on the hard ground.

Then the vehicle struck the fence and Joe was forced to look away, the light from the explosion momentarily blinding him. The ground shook and in its wake he heard the screech of falling metal. He looked to see one of the sentry towers toppling, tearing a hole in the fence as it fell. The mounted cannon exploded in a burst of energy, ripping a huge crater in the ground. Joe saw the Mariner defensive line scrambling back as another fence panel fell, crushing soldiers beneath it.

There was a cheer from out on the flats, echoing from

the dry slopes behind him. More vehicles broke from the central pack – Joe saw the Wildcats accelerating as they approached the breach in the fence, bouncing over the scorched ground. The second energy cannon was still firing, taking out a pair of lightweight squad cars. But a barrage of rockets from the speeding army slammed into the tower beneath it, weakening the struts. It swayed and groaned then it toppled forward, the cannon exploding as it struck the ground.

"This is bad," Black Crow muttered. "This is very bad."

A small, dented jeep came racing through the camp towards them, bouncing over the stony ground. It screeched to a halt and the rear door flew open, Nate scrambling out into the light. His skin was scorched red and Joe saw scars on his face that hadn't been there before. He pulled him in and they embraced, ignoring the din and the madness below them.

"What are you doing here?" Joe asked. "Why did The Five let you go?"

"Kara persuaded them," Nate explained. "I'll tell you all about it, but, Joe, we have to get to my aunt as fast as we can. I have a message for her, a time and a radio frequency. Kara said it was really, really… Mary?" He blinked as he saw Private Black Crow. "What are you doing here?"

"She's been helping me," Joe said. Then he looked up at his escort. "Will you take us to Nate's aunt? Can you drive us to Frisco?"

Black Crow looked doubtfully down towards the fence. Mariners swarmed into the breach, mounting a last-ditch defence as The Five's army drew relentlessly closer. General Jardine was barking orders into his radio, his face red with fury and disbelief.

"Will it help?" she asked. "Will it help us beat them?"

Nate nodded. "If we can get there in time, we might be able to make all this stop."

17
The Mariner Council

The cops picked Cane up at the Tower of Lost Children, hammering on her door as she struggled into her overalls. There were two of them, one tall and one broad, in blue-black uniforms with handguns in their holsters. Marco lurked in the corridor behind them, looking worried and half asleep. "What's this about?" he demanded. "Who gave your orders?"

The tall policeman shrugged. "We were told to bring her to the Council Chamber. Anything past that's not our concern."

"But why now?" Marco asked as they shoved past him, leading Cane to the elevator. "With this raider army advancing on the city, haven't you got better things to do than arresting teenage girls?"

"You'd think so," muttered the short cop.

"I'll come as soon as I can," Marco told Cane. "I'll find out what's happening and—"

"I don't need a babysitter," she told him. "Stay and look after the others – they'll need you if the raiders come."

The lift doors closed, the policemen standing silently as they descended to the lobby, ushering her through the sliding doors and into the foggy dawn. There was a patrol boat moored to the dock and she hunched in the back as they peeled away, ploughing through the still, shrouded water.

"Do you honestly not know what this is about?" she asked. "Who gave the order – my uncle?"

"It was Councillor Weaver," the tall cop said. "She told us to bring you in, quiet like."

Cane sat back feeling partly relieved, partly worried. She'd been wrestling with her conscience for days, half of her wanting to report what Rex had said, the other half scared stiff by her uncle's threats. If she betrayed her family a second time, she doubted even Sedna could keep her safe.

"Is there any news about the raiders?" she asked, trying to distract herself. "Have we turned them back yet?"

Word of the attack on Camp Badwater had broken the day before, spreading swiftly through the city. Everyone knew it would be dealt with quickly. No desert rabble could stand against the might of the Mariners. But still, it was the first time their defences had been breached.

"Last I heard they were still coming," the short cop said. "Past Modesto and moving west."

Cane's mouth fell open. "But those are residential zones. Why haven't they been stopped?"

The tall cop shrugged. "Maybe if your dad was in charge things'd be different. Hard to imagine him letting some band of mudfoots just walk in."

"My father fought one battle and lost," Cane bristled. "Trust me, he'd only make things worse."

They approached the Council Chamber, the plastiglass dome glistening through the mist. Surrounding it was a concourse dotted with trees, where loudspeakers relayed the day's debates to anyone who wanted to hear them. This morning the platform was packed, groups of Mariners standing silently in the fog, waiting anxiously for news of the invaders. The cops moored their boat to one of the jetties, ushering Cane towards the dome.

"I'm just saying we have to be prepared." The voice from the speakers was Sedna's, earnest and insistent. "Of course my honourable friend is right, we will repel these raiders before they reach the city. But how could it hurt to have our ships standing ready, in the unlikely event that an evacuation becomes necessary? The schools at least should be cleared."

"All right, all right." Rex's calm voice was unmistakeable. "If it'll soothe Councillor Weaver's fears, I will concede her point about the schools. But we cannot let fear drive our decisions. We need to rely on the information we have."

"And what information do we have?" This was a man's voice, quiet but edged with steel. Arthur Simwe, the Mariner president. "The reports I've received are patchy at best – we have no real idea how far this army has advanced overnight. They could be on our doorstep and we wouldn't know it until the cannons started firing."

People on the concourse glanced at one another, muttering fearfully. But Rex just laughed.

"That's impossible. Our troops are fighting for every inch of ground. I have no doubt that the next communication I receive will be from one of my commanders telling me the attack has been halted. We're the technological power here – they are desert rats in battered jalopies."

"Heavily armed desert rats," Sedna pointed out. "And surprisingly well organised. If I'm honest, my honourable friend's overconfidence recalls another member of his family."

There was murmuring from the other councillors and Rex growled angrily. "How many times do I have to remind the councillor that I am not my brother? I have distanced myself entirely from his actions, I have—"

"Very well," Sedna said wearily. "I withdraw the comment. Now if you'll excuse me, gentlemen, I have another important matter to attend to. I'll have those evacuation plans drawn up and ready to carry out by midday."

The cops led Cane across the concourse, but before they reached the building they turned aside, making for an arched opening where a flight of steps led down into the building's labyrinthine underchambers. From the surface the Council Chamber looked like a dome, resting on the surface of the water. But, in fact, it was a huge, half-submerged sphere, enclosed in a network of steel struts like an egg in a nest. The bottom half of the sphere was separated into several levels, linked by stairways and divided into offices and conference rooms. Through the transparent walls Cane could see aides busy at their work, computer screens flickering. The ocean surrounded them on all sides, and beneath her feet she could see a faint cylinder of shifting light as a tram passed through a tunnel.

"Wait here," one of the cops said, directing her into a small glass chamber with a desk and two chairs. They departed and Cane sat, the soft rush of the sea surrounding her. Looking up she could see through the reinforced ceiling to the central chamber where the councillors sat, dressed in their sea-blue robes of office. They were drawn from all walks of Mariner life, Cane knew – teachers and fisherfolk and soldiers.

But never forget, her father would always tell her, *these people may mean well, but they're politicians. They can't always be trusted, not with the tough decisions. Talking can only get you so far – sooner or later someone has to act.*

So how should I act now? Cane wondered. Should I betray you, Father? Or should I betray what I believe in?

"I'm sorry to drag you down here." Sedna's voice made her start, the old woman tucking her stick under her arm as she pushed into the office. "But there was something I needed you to see rather urgently."

She took a chair, activated a computer tablet and scrolled down until she found the right file. "This footage was taken approximately seventy minutes ago, just before dawn," she said, laying the tablet flat on the desk. "No one else knows about it apart from the governor of Alcatraz, myself and a handful of other councillors. I don't want to go public until I know precisely who's responsible."

The image was from a security camera, the footage grainy and indistinct. But Cane recognised the parking lot of Alcatraz prison, the outer fence and the entrance hall. Floodlights flickered and a familiar figure emerged through the reinforced doorway, hurrying across the concrete. She watched as her father jumped into a small amphibious vehicle, slammed the door and pulled away.

"Apparently he got hold of some newly developed computer virus that infected the security system," Sedna said. "Shut down all the locks, all the alarms. The guards went to secure the most violent offenders and he took the chance to escape. But here, this is from a few days ago. Look."

This time the image was of the meeting room at Alcatraz, a figure standing with her back to the camera. Cane recognised her own overalls, saw her father getting to his feet with a look of dismay. She turned but he called her back and they pressed their wrists together. Sedna froze the picture.

"We believe this was how he acquired the virus. It was masked to look like a financial transaction."

Cane gripped the edge of the desk. "I didn't know," she said. "You have to believe me. He said it was just for luxuries. I didn't—"

"Who said?" Sedna demanded. "Who gave you the virus?"

"I can't," Cane said. "They'll kill me if I tell you."

"I can protect you," Sedna insisted. "But I have to know. Whoever was behind this must have helped plan your father's attack on London, and organised the theft of the *Kraken*. And Cane, we have reason to believe they were also behind the pirate attack that killed my nephew and his friends. We believe they were trying to free your father before we could return him to Frisco."

Cane screwed up her eyes and for a moment it felt like the walls around her were cracking, the ocean rushing in to swallow her. Her mind swam, her thoughts were drowned, and it was all she could do to keep breathing.

Then she saw a face in her mind and fixed on it, hearing the echo of words from long ago. *You know what's right and what's wrong*, Kara had told her. *Maybe they'll try to tell you otherwise, but you're tough, you can handle it.*

"It was my uncle," she said, forcing the words out. "He's behind it all. He's not working alone – my family are in on it too, and some of the other councillors. But Rex and my father call the shots."

Sedna nodded kindly. "I suspected as much but it's good to have it confirmed. I'm just sorry you had to be the one to tell me. And I'm sorry your own family used you like this. It's monstrous."

Cane looked at the floor. "It's just what they're like. It's what I was like, too."

"Would you be willing to repeat all this to the Council?" Sedna asked. "Would you be willing to stand up and accuse your uncle of treason?"

Cane hesitated, then she gritted her teeth and nodded. "If he killed Kara, then I want to hear him admit it. And if my father's escaped, then people have to know."

There was a knock on the door and a young woman stepped in. "Councillor, I'm sorry but there's been an emergency transmission from a jeep crossing the Bay Bridge. It seems they escaped the attack on Badwater and now they want to meet with you, right away."

"With me?" Sedna asked. "I wonder what's going on."

She got unsteadily to her feet, leaning on her stick. Cane took her arm and they climbed the steps to the concourse where groups of Mariners still stood waiting for news. The mist was dense and coiling; Cane could feel it on her skin.

Past the dome a narrow slip road led down from the Bay Bridge, and on it they could see milky headlamps cutting through the fog. In the distance she thought she heard the rumble of thunder.

Then the shadows coalesced as a lightweight jeep pulled up, tyres screeching. The passenger door flew open and two small figures jumped out, running towards them. Sedna watched in disbelief, clutching Cane's arm with bony fingers. Cane felt her knees go weak, and had a sudden vision of the two of them falling flat on their backsides in surprise.

"Aunt Sedna!" Nate shouted, his voice echoing in the gloom. "It's us!"

"But…" Sedna managed, shaking her head. "But how is this possible?"

"It's a long story," Nate said, flinging his arms around her and squeezing as hard as he could.

"We floated to shore and got picked up by The Five," Joe said. "They brought us most of the way and after that, Private Black Crow took over."

"OK," Nate admitted. "Not that long."

Sedna seized Joe, rubbing his scruffy scalp with the flat of her hand. "Welcome to Frisco at last," she smiled. "And look, here's someone else to see you."

Cane's hands were shaking; she was almost too shocked to be happy. "Where's Kara?" she asked, peering through the fog towards the jeep. A young woman had climbed from the driver's seat but she had dark hair and a Mariner uniform. "Isn't she with you?"

"She sent me ahead," Nate told them. "With a message. We were hoping to arrive last night, but first we had a flat tyre, then we kept getting stopped at roadblocks. Not that they did any good. The Five managed to smash through every one of them. And now they're nearly here."

"We need to find a radio transmitter," Joe said. "That's what Kara's message was about."

"But there's hardly any time," Nate insisted. "They really are right be—"

There was a sudden flare of light, slanting through the fog across the Bay. It was followed by a deep, shivering boom, loud in the stillness. But this was no thunderstorm, Cane realised – the glow was tinged with red as the sound came again, followed by the crash of falling stone.

Nate gulped. "Right behind us," he finished.

18
Negotiations

The Five's army rumbled through the fog, down towards the Oakland shore. Through the train car's observation dome Kara could see trucks and assault cars rolling ahead, fractured stone buildings rising on either side. The sun was a pale smear, wisps of mist clinging to the glass.

They had advanced for a day and a night, cutting through the Mariner defences like a knife through water. The Five's opponents may have had the technological advantage but it had made them complacent – what fortifications the Mariners had were poorly manned, the men at the roadblocks entirely unprepared. At the first sign of trouble they scattered.

Things hadn't gone entirely to plan – early that morning the trucks had taken a wrong turn, smashing through a high wall into a stretch of grassy parkland. They were halfway across when someone in the train car had gasped and pointed, and Kara saw a huge shape keeping pace with them, ears flapping as the elephant stampeded through the fog. A hairy-headed ape had bounded on to the roof, thumping its chest and bellowing, and Kara had remembered Nate telling them about this many moons ago. *To the Mariners*, he'd said, *all life is precious. In Frisco we have zoos and sanctuaries with animals from all over the world.*

All life? Kara thought now. Really? They seemed to have taken much better care of the animals inside the fence than the humans outside it.

She wondered if Nate had made it back to his people bearing the message she'd given him. She wondered if anyone would listen even if he had. But most of all she wondered where Joe was and whether she'd made the worst mistake of her life letting him fly away.

"We're in position." Knuckles's voice brought her back to the present and she peered up through the glass roof. Above them hung a green sign with white arrows on it: BRIDGE AHEAD, it read, KEEP RIGHT. Beyond it the road sloped upward, vanishing into the fog. "All stop," he ordered into a radio handset. "Hold for instructions."

The trucks wheezed to a halt, their engines ebbing into eerie silence. Kara could hear the sea lapping on the shore up ahead, and all around them the

239

howling of escaped creatures.

Dash turned in his chair, facing her. "We're here," he said. "Are you ready?"

Kara nodded nervously as Knuckles reached for his transmitter and tuned the dial.

"What if your friend never made it?" Boxer asked. "Or if this Council of theirs won't listen?"

"Then we do it the old-fashioned way," Scar growled, slamming his fist into his palm. "I still don't know why we're bothering with any of this, jeopardising our entire operation on the strength of—"

"Because your brothers promised," Kara said. "Because I stopped Redeye from killing you. And because it's the right thing to do."

She took the handset from Knuckles, thumbing a switch on the side. "Nate, can you hear me?" she said. "Nate, come in please."

The only sound was static, and the thump of her heart.

"Can anyone hear me?" she went on. "Anyone at all, if you can hear me just—"

"Kara?" The voice was distant and crackling but she recognised it right away. "Kara, it's me!"

"Joe?" she almost shrieked. "You made it! Is Nate with you?"

"He's here," Joe told her. "And his aunt too. She

thought this might work better if everyone could see each other, so if you can broadcast pictures we should be able to pick you up on spectrum band 732.5."

Kara looked at Knuckles and he shrugged, rifling through a box of electronic equipment that he kept under his table. "I swear we've got an old camera around here somewhere."

"Joe, are you in one piece?" Kara asked. "I was so worried."

"It was really far," Joe told her. "I nearly got et by dogs, but I met Lenny who makes pictures, and I was at the camp when the trucks came. We got away and found Sedna and Cane."

"Hi, Kara." Cane's voice was full of relief. "I'm glad you're alive. I've got lots to tell you."

"Me too," Kara laughed.

Scar gave an impatient growl. "Enough of this schoolgirl chatter. Brother, what's the delay?"

"Got it," Knuckles said, plugging a dusty device into the console. He tapped on the keyboard and an image swam on to the screen, gradually sharpening. Joe leaned towards the camera, fish-eyed in the distorted picture. "We can see you," he said. "Can you see us?"

Kara waved a hand. "It's working."

Joe was standing in a large room beneath a curved,

241

transparent ceiling. Behind him were several tiers of benches occupied by silent, attentive Mariners. Nate poked his head in, then the camera turned and she saw Sedna standing beside a high podium made from crossed whalebones, her walking stick clutched in her hands.

"Kara, are these men with you?" she asked. "These Five that Joe has told us about?"

Kara stood aside as the clones arranged themselves into a line, identically expressionless as they faced the camera. Grey took a step forward. "We have agreed that I will do the talking," he said. "But know that when I speak, I speak for all of us. And for everyone who travels with us."

A man climbed on to the podium – he had a thin face and blue robes, staring resolutely into the lens. "My name is Alexander Simwe," he said. "I am the President of the Mariner High Council and leader of the Mariner movement worldwide. How should I address you?"

"We are The Five," Grey said. "Just The Five."

The President frowned. "Well, you are bold, I'll give you that. You've broken our defences, driven our troops back. But this is as far as you come. Every ship in Frisco Bay has its weapons trained on your position. If you attempt to advance, we will wipe you out."

Scar snarled. "We have a few surprises of our own. If you fire on us, we'll—"

"Brother," Dash interrupted. "We didn't come here to trade threats."

"Kara told us you were reasonable people," Grey said. "That you would be open to negotiation. Will you listen to our demands?"

Simwe hesitated, then he nodded. "Very well. But I promise nothing."

Grey drew himself up. "First, we want access to your technology. We want to see your records, your libraries. We want to know everything you know."

Simwe shook his head. "But that's—"

"Second," Grey said, cutting him off. "We want ships, or at least the means to build them. We intend for our nation to become a trading power and for that we need tankers, haulers, perhaps even an Ark of our own some day. And lastly, we need aid — not long term, just until we get on our feet. All across this continent people are starving — we need seeds and tools so we can start planting before the winter." He held up a hand, the fingers outstretched. "We will give you five minutes to formulate your response, then we will unleash our forces. Your time starts now."

He nodded to Knuckles and the connection was severed, the monitor screen going blank.

Dash looked at Kara. "Well," he said. "All we can do is hope."

* * *

Joe watched President Simwe as he stepped down from the podium, his fists clenched. "They're asking too much," he said. "Access to our records, use of our ships, it's impossible."

"I agree." Another man had joined them, broad and stocky with a bald head. "We should fire on them now, while they're not expecting it. Our ships are in position, we could use mounted cannons to—"

"Kara's with them," Cane protested. "Uncle Rex, you'd kill her too."

The bald man turned and Joe saw the family resemblance. So this was Cortez's brother.

"And besides, it's immoral," Sedna put in. "You can't agree to negotiate and then start shooting. It goes against every rule of decency."

Rex snorted. "Decency? These are desert creatures, the scum of the earth. They don't deserve decency."

"But that's why they're here!" Joe said, exasperated. "Exactly because of talk like that."

President Simwe squinted down at him. "What are you saying, child?"

Joe took a deep breath. "Councillor Sedna told us how some Mariners think. That not everyone deserves your help, that you should put your own needs first. But when

244

you act like that, this is what happens. People get angry, and pretty soon they come to your door with a big gun."

"Nonsense," Rex Cortez snapped. "This boy has no place in these discussions."

"Joe travelled with The Five," Sedna told him. "He knows what he's talking about."

"Then perhaps he's spying for them," Rex said to the president. "Have you thought of that? Why not turn him over to my men. They'll soon get to the truth."

"No!" Cane cried out. "You won't shut Joe up like you tried to do to me."

Sedna held her back as Rex turned, shock and anger warring on his face. He muttered a curse then he turned away, tugging a radio transmitter from his belt as he marched from the Chamber.

President Simwe frowned. "What was that?"

Sedna shook her head. "One crisis at a time," she said. "Go on, Joe."

He looked up at them. "I just think you ought to listen, that's all. Perhaps you don't have to do everything they want, but lots of it makes sense if you think about it. Would it hurt to give them seeds and tools, or lend them a few ships so they can trade? Even let them learn about some of the cool stuff you've got, like RPV and teethbrushes. Someone told me the other day that sometimes if you

245

help other people, you actually end up helping yourself. And that's good, isn't it?"

Kara stared from the dome as the seconds ticked by. The fog was beginning to dissipate, shafts of sunlight breaking through. Hearing howls, she looked up to see a family of monkeys taking refuge in the top of a nearby tower, as below them a spotted cat circled hungrily.

Then the radio crackled and Knuckles flicked on the monitor, watching as the screen wavered into life. President Simwe stood at the podium. His face was deadly serious.

"I have spoken with some of my … advisers," he said. "Five minutes is not long enough to formulate a detailed response. Any treaty will have to be thoroughly discussed and ratified by my fellow councillors before I can—"

"Get to the point," Grey cut in. "Is it a no or a yes?"

Simwe clasped his hands together. "We won't give you access to our weaponry," he said. "That technology will remain off limits. Any aid that we send will be strictly monitored to ensure that it goes to those who need it most – we won't have it ending up in the hands of petty warlords. But that aside, if you're willing to stand down your troops until we can work out the details, then … yes, I think we can come to an arrangement."

Kara felt a wave of relief rolling over her. Behind Simwe she could hear cheers breaking out – one of them was distinctly Joe's. Then just for a moment she heard other sounds – a distant shout and a muted pop.

Grey looked at his brothers. Dash nodded immediately, followed by Knuckles. Boxer glanced at Scar, who just stared back bitterly. Then he, too, nodded once.

"You have a deal," Grey said, turning back to the screen. "I'll tell our men we have agreed a ceasefire. But our forces will remain in place here until there's a clear plan to proceed."

"I suggest we send an envoy," Simwe said. "Councillor Sedna could meet you face to face to arrange further— What is going on back there?"

The President turned, looking over his shoulder. On the screen Kara could see figures moving behind him, hear shouts distorted by the bad connection.

"Excuse me," Simwe said. "There seems to be some kind of—"

There was a loud, percussive sound, making the speakers rattle. Simwe staggered, his eyes widening with confusion. He raised a hand and it was smeared with something, dripping from his fingers. He slumped from sight and Kara cried out.

"What's happening?" Grey demanded.

Kara heard more gunshots and the sound of shattering glass. Joe shouted "No!" as a figure approached the camera, shifting gradually into focus.

"There will be no ceasefire," a voice boomed through the speakers, grim and hard and horribly familiar. "There will be no negotiation and there will be no peace."

John Cortez faced the camera, a pistol in his hand. Behind him Kara saw armed men streaming into the Chamber. "You will take your army and leave, or you will be destroyed. That is our final offer."

He aimed his gun at the lens and fired, and the image turned to static.

19
Mutiny

Joe watched in horror as Cortez holstered his pistol, stepping over the lifeless body of the Mariner president. Soldiers streamed into the Council Chamber, rounding up the panicked politicians. Joe saw Rex barking orders, his loyal troops sealing the exits.

"John, what are you doing?" Sedna faced Cortez, her stick trembling. "You didn't have to kill him."

"But you left me no choice," Cortez replied, almost regretfully. "I didn't want to come here, I was to be smuggled out of Frisco entirely. But when Rex radioed and told me what was happening, how you were prepared to surrender to this scum, I knew I had to return. You don't negotiate with people like that, Sedna. There's only one language they understand, only one ... one— *Joe?*" He looked down in surprise. "Shark's teeth, it is you. And

249

the traitor boy, too. I heard you were lost at sea, along with…" He looked around worriedly. "Kara's not here, is she? That would be a bad omen."

"She's with The Five," Joe said. "That's how we got here."

Cortez laughed. "I should've known. I'll bet it was her idea to set up this little summit, wasn't it? Well, talking won't save her this time." He glanced briefly at Cane, shaking his head. "And you, daughter. Your uncle has told me of your treachery. We can deal with that later."

Cane clenched her fists and Joe could see the resentment behind her eyes. But Cortez had already turned away, taking Rex's arm and looking out across the Bay.

"What is our next move, brother? How do we deal with this rabble?"

Rex shielded his eyes, peering into the mist. "They have no ships," he said. "They'll have to come across the bridge. My instinct would be to blow it up ourselves, before they get the chance."

Cortez smiled thinly. "I like it. Sends a clear message that we're not messing around. Tell your ships to fire. We'll take out the bridge, then we'll pound them back into the sand."

Rex spoke into his radio and through the fog Joe could see the dark silhouettes of Mariner gunships, their cannons rotating into position. For a moment all was still.

Then there was a flash of white light and a colossal explosion, so loud that the dome itself shook. Chunks of concrete the size of houses went spinning into the air, lifted on a cushion of heat. The fog was driven back and waves crashed against the dome as the Bay Bridge collapsed span by span into the churning water.

Cortez watched, a faint smile on his face. "I was thinking," he said. "Once we've driven this rabble back into the desert, what's to stop us from following them? We could claim this entire continent for the Mariners. Get the mudfoots working for us, not against us."

"One thing at a time, brother," Rex replied.

Across the Bay Joe could see the ships turning, their guns training on the far shoreline. They fired and the sky lit up in blue and red, deep booms echoing through the glass of the dome. He gritted his teeth and prayed for Kara's safety.

"Full reverse!" Scar commanded, clutching the wall as the smoke from the broken bridge rolled back in a solid cloud. Trucks and cars slammed into one another as they tried to retreat, and beyond them on the water Kara could see the warships' guns locking into position, blue light flaring in the gloom.

251

The shoreline erupted, vehicles and entire buildings thrown into the air, rippling tides of pure heat rocking the train car as it reversed frantically towards a line of industrial buildings that stood back from the water. Sheltered behind them was a concrete lot and the army streamed in, engines grinding as the bombardment continued. Wild creatures fled into the mist, chattering and shrieking.

Scar turned on Dash. "Are you happy now? Didn't I tell you this would happen?"

"It was working," Dash insisted. "We were so close. If Cortez hadn't—"

"But he did," Scar snapped. "And now we're pinned down, out in the open."

"Enough bickering," Grey said. "We tried Kara's plan and it didn't succeed. I think it's time for our friends from Arizona to take their turn."

Boxer grinned savagely. "Yes," he said. "Tell them to rain fire."

Knuckles grabbed the radio. "Canyon Strike, this is Desert Command. The ceasefire is over and you are go for immediate deployment. I repeat, immediate deployment. Blow them to pieces."

Grey strode to the back of the train car with Scar at his side. Kara was close behind them, watching through the glass as the army retreated in disarray. At the rear of the convoy, out of range of the Mariners' weapons, she could see two hulking shapes – the trucks from Fort Coronado, dark in the smoky haze. Soldiers busied around them, hauling on thick cables.

The roof of the nearer truck began to slide open, a platform rising from inside. Standing on it was a jagged shape, all jutting angles and gleaming black steel, like some kind of nightmare insect. As Kara watched, four long blades emerged from its upper carapace and began to spin, slowly at first then with increasing speed. Dust rose and she could hear a deep, vibrating whirr.

"What are they?" she asked, as the second truck slid open and another shape emerged, its black shell lit by the explosions on the shore. "More flying machines?"

Grey nodded. "But these aren't chem-fuel rust buckets like the one Joe stole."

"These copters run on pure gasoline," Boxer said.

"Gasoline we provided," Knuckles added.

"And they pack a whole lot of punch," Scar grinned wolfishly.

The flying machines lifted, hovering above the trucks as soldiers gazed up in wonder. On the copter's side Kara saw rows of mounted guns and an array of finned missiles. The copters turned gracefully, banking in unison. Then their noses tipped downward and they surged forward, sweeping towards the Bay, their rotors driving a path through the smoke.

The Mariner ships raised their cannons, the barrels bursting blue. But the flying machines were too agile; they swerved clear, the energy bolts streaking uselessly into the sky. Kara saw the copters descending, missiles detaching and dropping towards the largest ship. Moments later its deck was torn apart in a flash of unbearable brightness.

"Strike!" Scar crowed, clapping Boxer on the back.

"Not so fast," Grey warned as two more ships began to turn, aiming their cannons at the swooping copters. They fired but again the flying machines were too nimble; another vessel burst into flame, men throwing themselves over the side as molten metal rained down.

Kara watched, panic rising inside her. Her negotiations had collapsed, Cortez had ruined everything. He would never surrender and neither would Scar. They would batter each other to pieces until the city lay in ruins, the army shattered. It was so pointless, so reckless, but what could she do?

Redeye's face flashed into her mind. He'd been ready to kill to keep this from happening, but she'd stopped him. Had he been right all along? Scar was so close, and in all this mayhem it wouldn't be hard to grab a gun. She could imagine the shock on his face as she pulled the trigger.

But even as the thought came she knew she couldn't do it. She was full of anger towards him but she knew that when the moment came she'd hesitate and all would be lost. Was that weakness? she wondered. Or was it goodness?

Suddenly, an understanding came to her. She'd watched The Five struggle to find balance, torn between their worst and their best instincts. This was just the same. *She* was just the same. The bad was inside her, the bitterness and the rage. It was the source of her frustration. It scared her sometimes but it also made her tough, made her a survivor. And of course the good was in there too, keeping her from going too far, reminding her of the right thing to do. She just needed to listen to it.

So what, she wondered, did the best part of her want? What did her decency desire most of all?

The answer was obvious. To end the war. And to find Joe.

And with that, a plan dropped into her head, fully formed the instant she thought of it. She opened her eyes in amazement. It was risky. It was a little bit mean. But it would work.

She got to her feet, taking Dash by the arm. "I need

to talk to you," she said, gesturing towards the stairs. "In private."

He looked back at his brothers but they were too busy giving orders.

"It's really important," Kara insisted. "I might have a way to stop all this."

Dash shook his head and followed her down. "It's too late for negotiations," he said. "Your friend Cortez won't listen. Anyway, he's a maniac."

"I know," Kara said, reaching into her jacket. She'd found the little pack of sleeping syringes that morning, the ones the doctor had given Nate but that he'd never used. She'd put them in her pocket along with the bandages from the bunker just in case things went bad.

Now she grasped one of the needles in her fist, flipping off the safety cap and turning to face Dash. She felt a moment's guilt, but it passed.

"I'm really sorry," she said. "But this is the best idea I've got."

She reached out and jabbed the needle into his arm.

Joe scanned the horizon as another warship exploded, the copters weaving like black birds of prey. Cortez watched in disbelief, his brother at his side.

"Why don't they blast them?" he seethed. "Why don't

they blow them out of the sky?"

"They're too quick," Rex said. "We don't have the tracking technology to follow something so small and light. There weren't supposed to be any machines like this left."

Nate leaned close to Joe. "What are we going to do?" he asked. "We can't stay here – it's going to get ugly."

"It's already ugly," Cane said, joining them. "Kara's plan was working until my father ruined everything. I hope she's all right."

"She will be," Joe said, looking at the smoke across the Bay. "She always knows what to do."

"Well, what would she do now?" Nate asked. "Where would she tell us to go?"

"The *Neptune* is standing ready." Sedna took hold of her nephew's arm. "I gave orders for it to be prepped as an evacuation ship."

Joe nodded. "Yes. That's what Kara would want. She'd tell us to get as far from here as we can, before—"

There was a cry and someone pointed up into the sky above the Bay. The Mariner fleet lay in ruins, smoke rising from the shattered hulks of their warships. And now the drone of the copters was growing louder as they closed in on the city.

"We need to leave," Rex said, grabbing Cortez by the

arm and tugging him towards the exit. "We're a sitting target. We have to move."

But it was too late. As the first copter drew nearer, Joe saw a missile detaching from its underside, tipping nose-down as it plunged for the dome.

There was a terrible, world-shattering noise, then darkness.

20

Islands

Kara had almost managed to haul her burden all the way to the yellow bus when a great cheer went up, and looking back she saw the Mariners' glass dome cracking open like an enormous eggshell. She lowered her head and quickened her pace, dragging Dash through the hills of rubble, his feet trailing on the ground. She'd thrown a shirt over his head and everyone around them was too busy to pay attention to her, but she knew it wouldn't be long before the chaos abated and the army was able to reorganise. They had to be gone before that happened.

She staggered up to the bus, reaching for the handle. But the door burst open suddenly and a figure emerged, blundering into her. Redeye jumped back, reaching blindly.

"Going somewhere?" Kara asked.

"You," Redeye said. "I see your little ceasefire plan went off smoothly."

"Everything was fine until Cortez showed up," Kara spat. "Honestly, all that work I put in, only to have it ruined by one meddling idiot."

Redeye shrugged. "Now you know how he felt, back in London."

Kara ignored this remark, looking around. "Where's Lynx? Is no one watching you?"

"That one ran off when the explosions started," Redeye said. "Gone to find the rest of the pussycat gang, no doubt. But what are you doing here? Come to make sure I'm in one piece?"

"Hardly," Kara said. "I've decided to deliver something to the Mariners. A gift."

Dash gave a sudden snore and Redeye jerked back in surprise. "Who's with you? Speak up!"

"He can't – he's unconscious," Kara explained. "It's my friend from The Five. He doesn't know it yet, but he's going to help me stop all this before the city gets flattened and Joe with it. There's just one problem."

"They blew up the bridge," Redeye said. "I heard it. And I'm the only one who knows the city."

"Is there another way across?" Kara asked. "Can you show me?"

"I might," Redeye said. "But what's in it for me?"

Kara sighed. "Really? How about you get to go back to your people, you get to humiliate The Five, and if you're really lucky I might even consider forgiving you."

Joe lay on his back feeling the floor tipping beneath him. The air was thick with smoke and all around him were pools of flame, casting everything in shades of dirty red.

He rolled over. The Council Chamber had been smashed open when the missiles fell, not just the dome but the walls and the floor too, great chunks of plastiglass dropping through into the offices below. Now the ocean was pouring in, gulping through jagged cracks in the side of the giant sphere. Beneath him he could see workers paddling desperately for the exits as the tide washed away desks and tables, filling the subsurface maze of rooms and hallways. Through a gap in the smoke he could see them scrambling up stairways, dragging each other to safety, swept along by the water.

And as the ocean rose, the floor beneath Joe started to float, the shattered surface separating into jagged fragments like miniature ice floes. He sat up carefully, finding himself in the centre of one of these broken islands. Nate lay nearby but there was no sign of Cane or Sedna; the smoke was too dense. He could hear screams in the fog and static hissing from the speaker system.

He reached out to touch Nate's shoulder and the boy sat up in alarm, the island rocking unnervingly. "Careful," Joe said. "We don't want to fall in."

Nate looked around, the reality of their situation sinking in. All was smoke and shadows.

Then the fog shifted, light cutting through. "Look!" Joe said, pointing. Some distance away was the bank of benches where the councillors had sat, the entire sloping structure fixed to the wall of the dome. At the top a door stood open, and people were escaping into the daylight.

But between them and the benches was an archipelago of floating glass islands, cracked and splintered and tilting. In the gloom Joe could make out a handful of figures slumped across them, councillors and Cortez's men, some lying still, others struggling for balance as the floes beneath them tipped. There was a shout as one of the soldiers lost his footing, sliding down into the swirling water. He tried to climb out but the glass was too smooth and too heavy, the floe rolling over and trapping the man beneath it. He kicked and struggled in the water, then he went still.

Nate's face turned pale. "We'll never make it. We'll drown."

Joe knelt, clutching the floor, his fears threatening to

overwhelm him. Nate was right. They'd probably die, either by fire or by water. Kara might never know what had happened to him.

But just the thought of Kara made Joe realise how far he'd come without her to protect him. Yes, he'd been scared almost all the time. But he'd done it anyway, travelling hundreds of miles across a wild, hostile continent. If he could do that, he could do anything.

"We can make it," he assured Nate. "We'll go carefully, take it one step at a time."

But the Mariner boy shook his head. "I'm not quick like you, Joe. I'll fall. I—"

Joe took his hand. "What did you tell Kara before? You're not scared like you used to be? I've seen it. It's true."

Nate blushed. "I thought so too. But maybe I was just acting brave to try and impress her. To make her… To make her like me. But it didn't work, so now I'm back to being scared stiff."

"Whatever the reason, you still did brave stuff," Joe insisted. "And if you want, when we see Kara again, I'll tell her you were totally fearless. I'll say you saved my life, like, six times."

Nate laughed despite himself. "I don't think it'll make any difference. But OK, tell me what I need to do."

They stood side by side in the centre of the floe. "I'll go first," Joe said. "I'll take one step forward then I'll jump over to that island, right there. You take a step back at the same time, then forward again, to keep it balanced. Does that make sense?"

Nate frowned. "I think so. Do a countdown so I know when."

Joe braced, counting from three. Then he took a quick step forward, the floor tilting sharply as Nate stepped back. Joe sprang to the next island, a larger one with the president's podium bolted in the centre. Then he turned, gesturing to Nate.

"Come on," he said. "I'll keep it steady."

Nate bobbed his head. "One step then jump," he muttered. "One step then jump."

He took a long stride then he leapt, the glass island tipping violently. He landed hard and staggered towards Joe, almost toppling him. But Joe held on to the podium and together they recovered their balance, clinging to one another.

Joe squeezed Nate's wrist. "I'd say six or seven more like that and we're safe."

Nate sighed. "Is that all?"

But the next jump was an easy one, the floor panel fixed to a supporting wall beneath. Under their feet Joe saw desks and chairs bobbing in the current, and darker shapes beneath.

As he leapt from that island to the next he found that he was starting to be able to gauge the balance points, where to stand as Nate hopped across to join him. And as they bounded on to another floe the smoke cleared again and they were able to see around the flooded chamber, the cracks in the ceiling, the barred lower exits, the curved benches rising in the gloom.

Then Nate's face fell and he pointed ahead. "How are we meant to get across that?"

Joe shielded his eyes. They didn't have far to go but between their island and the first row of benches was a sea of fragments, fractured plates of glass barely big enough to stand on. Peering up he saw a hole in the dome directly overhead. Part of the ceiling had dropped away, shattering as it smashed through the floor. And there was no way around it – to the right the wall rose sheer and smooth, to the left an exposed electric cable lay on a teetering island, sparking and twitching.

"We'll just have to go quickly," Joe said. "Jump from one to the next without stopping. Don't put your weight down for too long and I swear they'll hold you up."

Nate looked dubious. "You go first and I'll step where you step."

The cable flared, lighting up the patchwork of glass. Joe tried to plan a route in his head – that little one to that big one, then over to that tiny one. But if he put a foot wrong he'd be sunk, the densely packed islands making it all but impossible to climb back up.

He started out, stepping first on to a small floe barely bigger than his two feet, then on to a larger one where he paused and regained his balance. From there it was pure luck – he sprang from one island to the next, sometimes landing solidly, other times feeling the glass tip, forcing him to leap blindly, praying he'd have something to land on. His shoes were slippery, his arms spread wide as he hopped and bounded, barely daring to breathe.

Then before he knew it he was across, gripping the first row of benches as he clambered on to solid ground. He turned, beckoning to Nate. "It's not that bad," he lied. "You just have to keep moving. Use the same ones I used."

"I couldn't see which ones you used," Nate said plaintively. "It's too smoky."

"You can make it," Joe insisted. "And when it's done we'll be out."

Nate sighed. "Will you count me down? I find it helps."

Joe nodded. "Three," he said, hearing Nate hyperventilating in the darkness, "two, one, go!"

Nate jumped, landing on an island that tilted drastically

beneath him, sending him leaping to the left, waving his arms for balance. He landed and jumped again, giving a cry as the next floe flipped and he was thrown forward, one foot splashing momentarily into the water, the other landing hard on a stable platform. He found his equilibrium, breathing hard as he made another leap.

"You're so close," Joe said. "You're almost th—"

There was a splash as Nate hit the water, the island he'd tried to reach flipping right over and almost landing on top of him. He struggled, up to his neck, kicking frantically. Joe saw the loose electric cable rolling to the edge as the floes rocked and clattered.

"Stop kicking!" Joe shouted. "Keep your head up but don't move."

The glass islands were crowding around Nate; Joe heard him gasp and splutter as they pressed in, restricting his movements. Joe looked down – he could maybe cross the twenty feet of loose floes between himself and Nate, but could he pull the boy up? Any movement would be bound to rock the platforms, and that cable was ready to fall.

"You'll have to pull yourself out," he said. "I can't reach you. It's impossible."

"What?" Nate asked in horror. "I'm squeezed in. You have to come get me. You—"

He sank beneath the surface, waving his arms. The platforms around him jostled and Joe saw the cable roll, saw sparks fly as it slid towards the water. He cried out in helpless horror.

Then a boot came down and the cable was pinned in place, flickering and flaring. A hand reached out for Nate and a voice cried, "Grab on to me!"

Cane felt her fingers lock around Nate's wrist. She crouched on the edge of the unsteady platform, the cable trapped beneath her boot, sparking and hissing. In the flash, she saw Nate clawing with his free hand as he was dragged from the water, his knees finding the edge of the floe, coughing and gasping as he slumped down.

"You're OK," Cane told him. "I've got you."

"Attagirl!" Sedna called from the benches, hobbling towards Joe. "Now bring him over here."

Cane secured the cable then she helped Nate to his feet, one arm around his waist.

"I hope this makes up for the time I shot you," she said.

Nate looked up, his eyes wide. "Oh, we're definitely even."

Cane stepped across to the next island, reaching back to help Nate. Together they tottered across the last expanse of fractured floor, finally reaching the benches and scrambling on to firm ground.

"She's terribly impressive, isn't she?" Sedna said as her nephew fell gasping to his knees. "She saved my life too – I'd have drowned back there if it wasn't for her."

Cane felt herself blush. "It was nothing."

Joe looked around. "Where's your father? Did you see him again after the explosion?"

Cane shook her head. "He's either dead or he found a way out."

"My money's on the latter," Sedna said. "But, come on, we can still make it to the *Neptune*."

They emerged into daylight and Cane let out a gasp. The copters had bombed Frisco indiscriminately, smashing walkways and tearing the tops from tower blocks. Everywhere she looked she saw people in flight, either running towards the city in search of loved ones or away from it to save themselves. Smoke twisted and fires raged, reflected in a million fragments of shattered glass.

But in the distance rose a familiar shape – the *Neptune*, white chem-smoke already trailing from her funnels. "They've started the engines," she said. "Pier Nine. Come on."

They found a flight of steps and started down, curving around the cracked dome. But when they reached the main concourse, Sedna held back. "I can't leave," she said. "Not right away. I need to sound the evacuation, tell every Mariner to get to their ship."

"We'll come with you," Nate said. "We can send the signal then get to the Ark."

"No," Sedna told him. "I'd feel better knowing you were safe. I'll be there as quick as I can."

She pushed through the glass doors and back into the dome. Nate turned away and they sprinted across the concourse, the heat from a hundred fires filling the air.

Cane led them on to Embarcadero Walk, the towers casting long shadows across the broad steel gangway. Joe gazed up, awed by the soaring plastiglass blocks with their sheer sides and sloping roofs, many of them strung with climbing plants or inset with wind turbines and solar generators. Beyond them the shoreline rose through the smoke, the buildings of the old town blazing as the inferno spread. Cane wondered if she'd ever walk those streets again.

A siren blew, two short blasts then a longer one, echoing from speakers placed high on the surrounding buildings. The alarm was interspersed with a programmed voice repeating the same phrases over and over: "Evacuate immediately. Get to your ships. Evacuate immediately."

Many were already streaming from the towers, carrying

whatever they could. But as the siren sounded the flow of people increased, choking the walkway from end to end. Cane tried to force through, keeping low and fighting towards the docks.

"Hang on to me," she said as they reached Battery Circle, a floating hub where seven walkways branched like the spokes of a wheel. Here any sense of order had disintegrated, terrified Mariners shoving in every direction, surging senselessly. "We need to get across!" Cane shouted, gesturing to Pier Nine on the far side, the *Neptune*'s bulk rising between the towers.

"How?" Joe yelled over the shouts and sirens. "It's total madn—"

A shot rang out and a speaker on the wall exploded into fragments. The crowd scattered in terror, the platform clearing in seconds. In the centre a figure was revealed, regarding his fellow Mariners with disgust.

"Everybody, be calm!" Cortez barked, then he fired again, the reverberations echoing from the towers. "There's no need to panic. The situation is under control."

Rex stood at his side with a gang of surly-looking soldiers, their weapons drawn. Cane stared at her father, his lip drawn back in a disdainful sneer as he watched his people run for cover. Rage flared behind her eyes and she strode towards him.

"You're wrong!" she shouted. "Father, you're wrong. Anyone who stays here will die."

Cortez turned, raising one eyebrow. "Daughter. You're alive."

"We're going to the *Neptune*," Cane said, gesturing at Nate and Joe. "If you've got any sense, you'll come with us. This is another battle you can't win."

"Quiet, traitor!" Rex snapped, but Cortez held him back, his face softening.

"Cane, I don't have a choice," he insisted. "We're fighting for our very existence now. I know I failed you in London but, I promise, this time will be different. We'll be victorious."

Cane stopped, momentarily speechless. There were so many feelings battling inside her: frustration and sadness and a bitter kind of love, but most of all anger at his stubborn stupidity.

"You think that's why I turned against you?" she asked. "Because you *lost*? I turned against you because you did awful things, you murdered people, all for your own pride. And now you're doing it again. President Simwe was a good man, The Five were listening to him. Then you came along and ruined everything. Every single person who dies today, it'll be your fault. Because you're reckless and you've doomed our people."

272

Cortez took a single step forward and slapped her. Cane took the blow and it felt like a victory; at least she knew he'd heard her.

"You *are* a traitor," he hissed. "What kind of man would I be if I let them overrun this city? What kind of father would I be if I let them destroy our home?"

Cane cupped her cheek. Distantly she could hear the clatter of rotors.

"You're no kind of father," she said. "You never were. We loved you so much, Elroy and me. We worshiped you. And what did you do? You tried to drag us into your twisted schemes, tried to make us part of it. You used us. You killed my brother and you turned me into a criminal. You're—"

The explosion threw her off her feet, tearing out half the platform and the building beside it, showering glass and metal down around them. Cane tried to turn, to cushion the blow, but it was no use. Her head hit the floor, then there was nothing.

21
The Tram

Kara yanked the nest of wires from under the black steering wheel, slicing through them with a shard of glass. She twisted two together and the bus's engine fired, low and powerful.

"Quick work," Redeye said admiringly from the bench behind her. "You've had practice."

"Only on boats," Kara said. "Now, tell me how I work this thing."

Redeye's mechanical eye widened. "Wait, you've never driven before?"

"I'm from the Shanties, remember? Not a lot of buses around."

"But I assumed you'd... You were on the road with those..."

"Nope," Kara said. "So start teaching."

Redeye groaned, but it turned to hoarse laughter. "Oh, this is going to get messy."

He told her how to put the bus into drive and which pedals to push to get it started. The machine jerked forward, coughing and stuttering, but Kara got it back under control and began to ease between the piles of shattered concrete. Trucks and transports lay scorched and stalled around them, some still burning. On the bench beside Redeye, Dash stirred in his sleep.

"We'll make for the Golden Gate Bridge," Redeye said. "Head north. I'll direct you."

Kara gripped the wheel, aiming for a gap between two smouldering lorries. Beyond them was a stretch of open road. "You know, this is actually easier than it—"

"Hey!"

Lynx leapt into the bus's path and Kara braked instinctively. Redeye pulled Dash down in his lap, covering the clone's head and trying to look innocent.

"Where do you think you're going?" Lynx tugged on the door but Kara had forced a spike of metal into the mechanism and it was wedged tight. "Did someone say you could leave?"

"You don't need us," Kara shouted back. "Why not just let us go?"

"Because he's The Five's prisoner," Lynx said, straining

275

on the handle. "And you're … whatever you are. It's for the bosses to decide who stays and who goes, so step out of the vehicle."

Kara shook her head. "I'm sorry," she said, "I can't."

"I knew you were trouble," Lynx snarled. "From that very first day, I knew it. And now you've ruined everything with your meddling and your— Who is *that*?"

Lynx pointed through the crack in the door, eyes wide with astonishment. Dash was struggling upright, blinking blearily as Redeye tried to shove him back down. The clone squinted at Kara, then seemed to decide he was still dreaming and lay back in Redeye's lap, snoring softly.

"Kidnappers!" Lynx screamed. "Traitors!"

In the mirror Kara saw Leo and Tigress sprinting towards the bus, weapons drawn. She slammed her foot on the throttle and the bus jerked forward, engine grinding. Lynx clung to the door, yelling indistinctly as the wheels crunched over piles of fallen concrete. Kara aimed for the open street, pressing hard on the pedal, forcing the smuggler to let go. The last thing she saw as the bus powered away was Lynx sitting in the dirt, one fist waving, steel teeth flashing in the gloom.

Joe staggered to his feet, coughing dust. He felt a pain in his neck and reached up, pulling out an inch-long splinter of glass with blood on the tip. One shoe had been knocked off and he reached out to retrieve it. The platform around him was littered with wreckage.

A cry cut the air and Nate sat up, looking around blearily. Across the circle Joe could see the hunched figure of a man, kneeling over a scorched body that lay twisted on the steel.

Cortez.

And Cane.

Her father raised his head and howled again, a wrenching wail of absolute despair. Joe took a step towards them, so unsteady that he almost fell. Cane lay with her eyes wide, her clothes and her hair still smoking from the blast. Her arm was twisted beneath her and there was blood on her face. Joe knew right away that she was dead.

Suddenly an image came to him from long ago. A young man, blistered from an explosion, lying on a blackened platform. Cane's brother, Elroy. Joe had been powerless to save him, too.

Cortez shook his daughter, whimpering. His face was a mask of grief, tears streaming from his bloodshot blue eyes. In that moment he looked almost human.

Rex looked down, emotionless. "I'm sorry, John," he said. "She didn't deserve this."

"Don't be sorry," Cortez screamed, clutching her. "Fix it! Make them pay. Every scum-sucking last one, make them die in agony."

Rex blinked. "How?"

"Assemble our forces," Cortez said, placing Cane down on the platform and staggering to his feet. "Anyone who can fight, old men, boys, girls. We'll drive them into the desert, then we'll bomb the desert. We'll track down anyone who ever helped them, anyone who ever supported them, and—"

"Weren't you listening?" Joe shouted, unable to stay quiet any longer. "Didn't you hear anything Cane said before she… Before…" He bunched his fists, trying to keep himself from screaming, all too aware of the broken figure lying on the boards between them. "She said you were *wrong*. She said you were a killer. You can't fix this with more killing."

But Cortez barely seemed to hear him, turning to face his men. "Shut down that evacuation siren," he ordered. "The old woman might try to stop you – kill her if you have to. Then—"

Joe marched forward and grabbed his arm, yanking it hard. "No!" he shouted. "You have to listen to me. We've seen The Five's army. There are too many of them. We came all this way to save the Mariners, but if you fight and you lose, that's all for nothing. They'll storm this city and kill anyone who stands against them. Do you think that's what Cane would have wanted?"

"Don't tell me what she'd have wanted," Cortez spat. "She was a fighter – she wouldn't have run away, not in the end. These mudfoots murdered my child. I will not let them—"

"The boy's right, John."

Joe turned in surprise. Rex was squinting up at his brother. "I know it doesn't feel like it, but he's right. Our loyalty was never to this place, to this patch of land. It was always to the Mariners, to the cause, to the dream. If we fight and The Five win, that dream dies. We have to save what we can and go."

"Run away?" Cortez asked bitterly.

Rex nodded. "We've lost the battle, but we can still win the war. We can avenge your daughter, and ensure a future for our people. Remember the transition zone, John. Remember Plan B."

"Plan B," Cortez repeated, and Joe saw a cold light dawning in his eyes. "*Yes.*"

Then all of a sudden he seemed to snap into focus, brushing back the tears with a sweep of his hand and turning to the mercenaries gathered round him. "Change of strategy," he said. "We evacuate on the *Neptune*." And he strode away, heading for the harbour.

"Wait!" Joe called, gesturing to the girl who lay sprawled in the sunlight. "What about your daughter?"

But Cortez barely glanced back. "Let them look into her face," he said. "Let them feel shame for what they've done." Then he was lost between the buildings.

Joe looked at Nate, unable to comprehend what had just happened. He'd heard the pain in Cortez's cries. He knew how deeply the loss had wounded him. But then he'd just … what? Shrugged it off, forced it down? It was a kind of strength Joe couldn't begin to comprehend.

"We can't leave her," he said, crouching beside Cane and forcing himself to look. Her expression was calm; there was blood in her hair and a little on her face, but otherwise she could've been sleeping.

Nate nodded. "She's a Mariner. There's only one place for her."

Joe knew what he meant, and he knew it was true. Cane was a child of the ocean – it had nurtured her all her life. It was only right that she return to it now. Not that anything about this was right.

They lifted Cane carefully to the edge of the platform then they placed her gently into the water, standing hand in hand on the edge. Cane's arms drifted upward as she descended, her hair like a halo as she sank out of sight.

Joe bowed his head for a moment, his vision blurred by tears. Then Nate tugged his hand and they turned away, staggering, then breaking into a run.

The suburbs were crowded as the bus rattled north, fishtailing round a tight bend and sideswiping parked vehicles on both sides of the street. Kara thought she was getting the hang of it though – she'd smashed both headlamps and there was a big dent in the side from when she'd accidentally run into a tree, but the engine was still running and they were all unharmed.

The roads were narrower here, lined with stores selling clothes and music and the latest sailing tackle. Evacuation sirens blared and Mariners came streaming from their homes and office blocks, hurrying down towards the busy shoreline. Kara blew the horn and tried not to hit them.

"Why are they still here?" she wondered. "Why didn't they leave already?"

"Because they thought they'd win," Redeye said. "We Mariners have a tendency to think we're better than everyone else. Of course, it's usually true."

Hearing a groan, Kara glanced in the mirror. Dash was stirring again, his eyelids fluttering.

"If he wakes up you need to hold on to him," she told Redeye. "We don't want him making trouble." Then she saw movement in the mirror and her heartbeat quickened. "We've got enough of that as it is. Hang on."

A car was gaining on them, flanked by two more. The Wildcats rocketed down the busy boulevard, scattering pedestrians. Kara floored the throttle and a pair of passers-by leapt clear. But there were many more up ahead and she couldn't bear the thought of running someone down.

Seeing an opening, she yanked the wheel and the bus skidded sideways, slamming into a narrow alleyway, the side mirror flying off in a spray of sparks. They hurtled along, bags of rubbish bursting under the wheels, a startled cat yowling as it leapt aside.

They broke out into a wide green square and Kara shifted gears, bouncing them up over the kerb and on to the grass. But the Wildcats were still gaining, their engines faster and more powerful. It wasn't long before Lynx drew level, leaning out to yell at Kara. "You can't outrun us, you know. Not in that hunk of junk."

Kara wrestled with the wheel, congratulating herself as they swerved around a clump of trees. In the mirror she could see Tigress following, tyres churning up the grass. Where's Leo? she wondered as they thumped back on to the tarmac and into another wide street, Lynx's car still neck and neck.

The smuggler grinned through steel-capped teeth as the two vehicles ground together, sparks flying. "You're enjoying this," Kara called out in amazement.

Lynx laughed. "Ain't you? Come on, have a little fun!"

Kara shook her head in disbelief, trying to focus on the road ahead. Suddenly Lynx hit the brake, swinging in behind, and Kara frowned in confusion. She didn't see Leo's huge off-roader as it screamed towards them and slammed into the side of the bus.

Kara clung to the wheel as they corkscrewed across an open intersection, tyres exploding, the bus leaning steeply as it spun. She heard herself cry out as it tipped door-side down, glass and sparks flying. Then they scraped to a standstill, smoke pouring from the engine.

Kara clung to her seat belt, looking down to see Redeye sprawled below her on a bed of glass. Dash lay outstretched on top of him, still unconscious. "Are you hurt?" Kara asked.

Redeye checked himself. "I don't think so. Just a few cuts and b—"

With a shout Dash woke up, kicking wildly. Redeye yelled in surprise and Dash staggered to his feet, blinking in confusion. "Wh—" he managed, touching his face as though checking it was still there. "What's happening? Where are my brothers?"

"They're not here," Kara told him as Redeye stood shakily, taking hold of the clone. "I'm sorry, but we've kidnapped you."

Dash looked up at her in horror. "Kidnapped? But I need to get back. They'll be—"

"That's not possible," Kara told him. "If you try to run away, Redeye will stop you. He's blind, but he'll do his best."

Redeye stuck his hand in his pocket as though he had a pistol. "I promise not to hurt you," he said, "as long as you do as I say."

"As *we* say," Kara corrected him. "Well, as I say, actually."

Dash stared up at her, terror gleaming in his eyes. "Kara, I haven't been apart from my brothers since … well, ever. I thought you understood. I thought we were friends."

"We are," Kara said, as engines rumbled in the street outside. "And as my friend, you're helping me escape. Now come on, we'd better move."

She unhooked her belt and climbed from the driver's side window, helping Dash and Redeye up behind her. As they dropped to the tarmac she saw the Wildcats a short distance away, advancing cautiously through a carpet of broken glass.

The street was lined with houses, many of their doors standing open. Kara ran for one, leading the others inside. A small dog yapped but she ignored it, pushing through a kitchen with pictures of sailing boats on the walls and out through the back door. Down a long, sloping street she could see the ocean, sparkling blue between the buildings. Light flared and smoke rose from the distant city.

"Where do we go from here?" she asked Redeye. "How far's this Golden Gate?"

"Too far," he admitted. "We won't make it on foot."

"So we head for the water," Kara said, looking at the shoreline dotted with white boats. "We steal a ship, hope no one tries to—"

"Wait," Redeye said, holding up a hand. "I've got a better idea. Listen."

Kara tipped her head. Beneath the wail of the sirens and the thrum of Wildcat engines she could hear a lighter sound: a bell ringing. "This way," Redeye said, pulling Dash with him.

The street was wide with trees planted down the centre. The bell was louder now, clanging towards them. Kara turned to see a crimson vehicle rattling into view, running on silver rails. It was shaped like a box on wheels, the windows and the footplates crowded with frightened Mariners.

"What does it say on the front?" Redeye asked.

"Pier Ten," Kara told him. "Is that good?"

"It's perfect. Climb on."

"But it's full," Dash said as the tram slid past. "We'll never fit."

Redeye frowned. "Look on the back. There should be a handrail, do you see it?"

Kara scanned the vehicle's rear; there were two steel buffers and a single window, and above it a small steel bar. "It's there but it's tiny. We can't all hang on."

"But we can climb up," Redeye said. "Me and Elroy used to ride the roof all the time. The conductors hated it but right now I think they'd let it go."

They jogged behind the tram as it glided down the hill. Kara climbed on first, hauling herself up by the railing and turning to grab Dash's hand. Redeye followed and they clambered on to the roof, ducking beneath the thick steel cables suspended overhead. In the centre was a nest of sparking wires, and Kara could feel the electricity in the air.

Hearing engines, she looked back up the steeply sloping street. The Wildcats took a tight corner behind them, skidding as they came. The tram descended towards the seafront but the cars were much faster, Lynx glaring furiously through the windshield as they closed the gap.

The cars swung in from both sides, Lynx and Leo harrying the tram, making it shudder and screech. Inside the passengers cried out, their screams amplified in the narrow space. Then the tram began to slow, brakes whining. "What's it doing?" Kara cried. "Don't stop!"

Redeye reached out blindly, fumbling for an electrical junction box bolted to the roof, from which a hooked pole connected to the cables overhead. He wrenched open a panel, frowning with concentration. "This is another old trick of Elroy's. Hang on."

He yanked a cable loose then he shoved it back into the junction box, sparks lighting up his face. There was a clunk and the tram began to accelerate, shops and houses flying by. There was another chorus of shrieks from below.

The ocean was ahead of them now and Kara wondered which way the tram would take them — south or north? Either way the bend would be tight — she hoped they didn't come off the rails.

Then she saw a metal arch rising, the rails vanishing into the dark. Suddenly Redeye's plan made sense.

The Wildcats braked hard, falling in behind the tram. They were still picking up speed as they shot into the tunnel, Kara's ears popping as pressure hit them from both sides. The sound of the wheels changed from a distant whine to a clattering rumble and she felt a sudden rush of claustrophobia, remembering that awful subway beneath London, deep and dark and full of spiders.

But this tunnel wasn't dingy; it was clear-sided and luminous, sunlight rippling down through the water. Boats drifted overhead, black against the green sea. Schools of fish darted in the depths, undisturbed by the madness above.

"Look at this place," Dash marvelled. "It's incredible." His initial panic seemed to have abated and he was showing few signs of trying to escape.

"And just think," Redeye said. "You and your brothers wanted to blow it all up."

"No," Dash turned to him. "We never wanted that. Or at least I didn't. We just want the chance to make things like this for ourselves. We want your people to share what they know."

"And if they don't, you'll kill them."

Kara barked a laugh. "Now who does that remind me of? You're all as mad as each other."

The tracks levelled out, the tram speeding through the aquamarine light. Then the chassis shook and she looked over the back, seeing Lynx's car nudging against the buffers. The other Wildcats were lined up behind, Leo hunched over the wheel, Tigress leaning from her window clutching a pistol. She fired but her aim was

288

poor; the shots ricocheted off the ceiling.

"She can't crack the tunnel, can she?" Kara asked worriedly.

"Not with a handgun," Redeye said.

Dash let out a whimper. "How about with a grenade launcher?"

Leo had hoisted himself up on to the driver's side window, keeping the big vehicle steady with his foot. On his shoulder was balanced a long black tube with a firing mechanism at the rear end.

"He's crazy!" Kara exclaimed.

Dash shook his head. "No. Just really stupid."

Leo squinted as the car jerked beneath him. He fumbled for the trigger, swerving slightly, tyres grinding against the tramrails. Kara heard a clunk as they crossed a junction, the tram veering left. Lynx steered through but Leo didn't see it, his car bouncing hard as it slammed over the rails. His finger squeezed instinctively and fire burst from the launcher's barrel, the kickback sending him flying from the car. The spinning grenade missed the tram by metres, shooting towards the ceiling.

Kara held her breath but the tunnel didn't crack. The grenade struck it and dropped back vertically, missing Lynx's car by a whisker and exploding on the tracks. The fireball ripped through the tunnel, slamming the tram forward.

Kara lifted her head to see Leo's car rolling sideways, the tyres and the windshield bursting in the heat. It landed upside down on the tracks and Tigress braked desperately, careening into it in a confusion of metal and flying glass. Through the smoke Kara could see Leo picking himself off the floor of the tunnel, then sitting back down again with his mouth open.

Kara shook her head. "What an idiot. Still, it's perfect for us. He's managed to——"

Lynx's car slammed into the tram and she was taken by surprise, losing her grip and tumbling over the back, clawing at nothing. Kara landed flat on her back, the air knocked from her. Looking up she could see the roof of the tunnel flying past, Dash's startled face looking down. She was splayed on the hood of Lynx's car, her feet on the cracked windshield, her head smacking from side to side as the smuggler twisted the wheel, trying to shake her loose.

"Grab my hand!" Dash shouted, reaching down as far as he could. Kara tried to roll over but her jacket was snagged on the radiator grille, tearing as she tried to steady herself. The car weaved along the tunnel, bumping over the rails, the walls on either side turning pale. She clung on, gritting her teeth as they shot out into the daylight.

22
Evacuation

On the pier beside the *Neptune* everything was in chaos. The gangplanks had been lowered and people were streaming on board, carrying whatever they could – children, pets, precious possessions. The Ark was huge, Joe knew, but there seemed no end to the number of evacuees. Ahead and behind he could see more ships, smaller frigates and transport vessels, plus another Ark that Nate told him was the *Neptune*'s sister ship, *Poseidon*. Others had already left port, steering out into the Bay.

As they reached the gangway, Joe saw Cortez at the top, shouldering into the hangar. He was like a machine, emotionless and determined. Joe remembered the way he'd marched past Cane's body, hardly even looking back. He felt a wave of sickness and sadness, unable to believe she was gone. He shook his head, trying to fix on the present, but he kept seeing her face in his mind.

"We'll wait here for Aunt Sedna," Nate said. "We'll only go up at the very last minute."

Joe climbed on to the sea wall, scanning the crowd for any sign of the old woman. He'd never imagined there were so many Mariners, as many as there were people in the Shanties, maybe more. He remembered that night on the Pavilion when he'd searched in vain for Kara, and wondered where she was now. With The Five no doubt, probably still trying to reason with them. Back across the Bay he could see movement around the base of the broken bridge, and the flash of intermittent gunfire. The clones must be seizing ships to ferry their men across. Soon they would storm the city.

The *Neptune*'s front gangplank started to retract and, looking up, Joe saw figures crowding the higher decks, faces framed in every porthole. The ship was getting full. Then he heard the screech of metal and turned back, shielding his eyes.

On the docks beside the pier was the entrance to a tunnel. Local trams had been emerging regularly, their passengers shoving for the ships. He could see another one now, rattling through the archway, crammed like the others. But this one was moving much faster, sparks flying as it rocketed on to the dock. There was another vehicle behind it; a mud-coloured car with something on the hood. He looked closer. It couldn't be.

"That's Kara," Nate said in amazement. "What's she doing?"

The crowd began to cry out, shoving back as the tram hurtled along the dock. Dropping from the wall Joe broke into a run.

"Look, on the tram," Nate said, struggling to keep pace. "Is that one of The Five? And there's someone with him. I can't... No. No, it's *impossible*."

Redeye crouched, the cables whipping over his head. Dash was leaning over the back, hands outstretched towards Kara. But no one was watching where they were going, and as he turned to look, Joe's heart seized.

The tram was approaching the end of the dock, where the rails took a sharp bend and doubled back towards the tunnel. "Hey!" he screamed, waving his arms. "One of you, look!"

Redeye raised his head blindly, recognising Joe's voice. He reached back and tugged on Dash's sleeve and the clone turned, his jaw dropping. Joe screamed Kara's name but she was too far away and the engine was too loud. The tram hit the bend at full pelt, two wheels leaving the track as it cornered wildly. Dash and Redeye clung on, the passengers inside howling with terror.

293

But Lynx had seen nothing, too distracted by the obstacle on the hood. The car flew off the end of the dock, Kara spread-eagled as they hit the water, sending up a fountain of spray. Joe ran to the edge, watching the car flip over and sink. Kara was driven down beneath it.

He tore off his jacket and kicked off his shoes, jackknifing into the water. It was warmer than he was used to, and clearer too. Below him he could see the outline of the car, bubbles trailing as it plunged downward. It had started to level out, drifting roof-down towards the base of a tower sunk into the sea bed.

He could see Kara too, and to his relief she was moving, clinging to one of the wheels with her feet braced against the driver's side window. She kicked, trying to break the glass and get to Lynx. But it was too thick and the car was still sinking, forcing her to hang on.

Joe swam towards her, putting on a burst of speed. Kara jumped as he took hold of her shoulder, pulling her round. Then she hugged him, the breath almost driven from Joe's lungs as she squeezed him tight.

She pulled away, gesturing to her mouth; she was running out of air. She pointed to the car as it finally hit bottom, resting wheels-up on the concrete foundations of the tower block. Lynx was trapped inside, eyes lightly closed, suspended head-down by the seat belt. But the ocean was pouring in, a deepening pool filling the roof. Lynx's forehead was already under; there wasn't much time.

Joe reached into his pocket, pulling out his shard of metal, the one he'd found in the dust all those days ago. He pointed to the lock, turning the pick in his hand. Kara nodded.

He held her steady as she inspected the lock, fighting to stay focused. She poked with the metal, missed and tried again, working it in and twisting it round. The lock clicked and Kara reached for the handle. But her fingers slipped and Joe felt her body go slack, drifting away from him.

He pulled her close, squeezing her wrist as hard as he could, but it wasn't enough. Kara's eyes rolled back in her head, her arms limp at her sides. Then he remembered something an old Beef had told him back when he was just a kid. He'd always found the idea disgusting, but if it worked...

He forced Kara's mouth open and stuck two fingers inside, jamming them as far as he could. She jerked awake immediately, trying to cough but her mouth was full of water. Joe shoved her up, pointing to the surface. Kara began to kick, rising into the shimmering light.

Now Joe felt his own lungs burning; he didn't have long.

He tugged on the door but the hinges were stiff and his arms were weak. His vision was starting to narrow and he fixed on Lynx, tightening his grip on the handle. After Cane, after everything, he refused to let another one go.

Just the thought of Cane seemed to lend Joe strength and he tugged as hard as he could, wrenching the door open. Lynx's belt was strapped tight so he scrabbled for the mechanism, the smuggler's head lolling against his neck. After a moment's fumbling the strap came loose and he hauled Lynx out of the car, feeling the weight as they began to rise. The surface was a long way off but somehow he found the determination, his eyes wide and stinging.

Then there were hands on him, Kara pulling him up the last few metres. They broke the surface together, bursting into sunlight. Kara grabbed him, kissing his face as Lynx bobbed beside them. "You saved me," she spluttered.

"I know," Joe smiled. "Usually it's the other way round isn't it?"

Lynx was still unconscious as they clambered from the water and laid the smuggler down. Kara leaned in, pressing her lips to Lynx's and breathing hard. She pumped Lynx's chest but there was no response; their face was ashen and their hands were motionless.

"I don't think—" Joe began but Kara shook her head.

"Lynx is tough," she insisted. "A fighter."

She raised a hand, whispering, "I'm so sorry," as she dealt Lynx a hard slap, then another. Joe winced as Kara drew back a third time, but the slap never landed.

A hand shot out, grabbing Kara's wrist. Lynx coughed seawater and struggled up.

"You're OK," Kara said. "It's—"

Lynx lunged for her, wrapping both hands around Kara's throat and squeezing. Kara tried to pull away but Lynx's grip was too strong, eyes wild with confusion and fear.

"Stop!" Joe shouted. "She just saved your life!"

But Lynx wasn't listening, shaking Kara fiercely as she kicked and fought.

Then someone else broke in, reaching down and taking Lynx firmly by the arm.

"Release her," Dash said. "That's an order."

Lynx let go immediately, looking up in astonishment. "Y-you! But why… After she…"

"I know," Dash said. Behind him the tram had been brought to a halt, the terrified passengers disembarking shakily. "Kara kidnapped me. At first it seemed like a mean trick. But then I thought about it, and … well, she's got pretty good reasons. If she can persuade my brothers to stop the bombing, if we can make this end, then maybe it's worth it."

"But we came here to crush them," Lynx said. "You… The Five… That's what you wanted."

"My brothers, perhaps," Dash said. "But Kara showed me… Well, she helped me see that what *they* want isn't always what *I* want."

Lynx stared at him speechlessly, as though the world had just flipped upside down.

"I know it's a lot to take in," Kara said sympathetically. Then she pointed to the *Neptune*. "We're getting on that ship, and he's coming with us. If you want, you can come too."

Lynx turned on her. "I serve The Five. I always will."

"But one of The Five is here," Dash pointed out. "And I could probably use a bodyguard."

"We might all need one now that Cortez is back in charge," Kara said.

"But I can't leave my friends," Lynx said, faltering. "And I won't betray your brothers."

"I know it feels that way," Dash said. "But I promise, if they were here, they'd tell you to go with me. Lynx, I don't know what's going to happen. I've never been alone before and I'm scared. But I trust you, and I'm asking for your protection. Please."

Lynx stared at him, eyes filled with uncertainty. Then the smuggler sank back, muttering a curse. "If anyone asks, you all forced me. At gunpoint."

Kara clapped Lynx on the shoulder. "It's a deal. Now let's move."

They ran for the Ark, reaching it just as the last gangplank was about to be raised. Kara went first, leading Dash. We made it, Joe thought as he hurried after them. It was impossible but we made it.

Then he felt a hand on his arm and turned. Nate had stopped at the foot of the plank, looking scared but determined, as though he'd just come to a difficult decision.

"I can't go," he told Joe. "Not without Aunt Sedna. She came all the way to London to get me. The least I can do is wait for her."

"The Five are on their way," Joe protested. "You'll be captured."

"I've been captured before," Nate said. "And hey, maybe it'll be good to have someone here on the inside. Keeping an eye on them."

"But we've come so far together," Joe argued. "You and me and Kara. We need y—"

"Don't say it," Nate told him. "You don't need me, and Kara certainly doesn't. I'll see you both again, I promise.

299

And I'll think about you every day. I'm a different person because of you two."

Joe smiled. "I think that's true. The old Nate would've been first up this gangplank."

The Mariner boy laughed. "Look after Kara. I know she doesn't need it, but do it anyway. Tell her ... well, tell her I love her, I guess."

Joe felt the gangplank rising beneath him and scrambled upward. "I will!" he shouted, darting through the hatch just as it slammed shut.

Kara pushed through the teeming hangar, leading Dash by the arm. The floor began to rumble as the engines powered up. The Ark was on the move.

She spotted Redeye by the elevator and crossed to join him. Joe slipped inside just as the lift doors slid shut. "Where's Nate?" Kara asked him. "Still in the hold?"

Joe shook his head. "He stayed behind. He gave me a message, but I'll tell you later." Then his face turned serious. "Listen, Cane didn't ... she didn't make it. There was an explosion. She died."

Kara gasped and Redeye stared at Joe in sightless disbelief. "That's impossible."

"I was there," Joe said. "I saw it."

"But I had..." Kara screwed up her eyes, trying not to

let her emotions overwhelm her. "I had so many things I wanted to say to her."

"She stood up to her father," Joe told them. "She yelled right in his face, told him he was wrong. It was amazing. But then … then she… I thought, if you're going to speak to him, you should know."

Redeye slumped against the wall of the elevator. Kara wiped her eyes roughly with her sleeve, gritting her teeth so hard it hurt. "It's awful, but it doesn't change what we came here to do," she said. "There are still plenty of other people who need our help."

They emerged on to the upper deck, turning towards the bridge. From inside, Kara could hear Cortez barking orders and she felt her chest tighten. How had it come to this? Still, for now all that mattered was bringing an end to the destruction.

Ahead of the Ark she could see a red bridge spanning the horizon, towers reaching to the sky. Beneath it a line of Mariner ships trailed into the open ocean. But as she watched, the copters swooped down and one of the boats vanished in fire and steam.

"They're coming around," an officer was saying as Kara stepped on to the bridge. "I think they've spotted us."

"Ready weapons," Cortez ordered. "Tell them to bring

those machines down before they—"

"We've got a better idea," Redeye said, and Cortez turned.

"By jaws," he said. "My old friend. We'd given you up for dead."

"Have the reunion later," Kara said. "We've got bigger issues."

"Kara," Cortez hissed. "What do you think you're doing?"

"Saving your life," she said. "I'm just sorry I was too late to save Cane."

Cortez's mouth tightened. "Don't you speak my daughter's name." Then his gaze fell on Dash and he stepped forward, eyes flaring. "You dare to bring one of those … creatures on to my ship?"

Kara stood protectively in front of the clone. "He's my prisoner. And now I need a transmitter, tuned to… What was it again? 732 point something."

"Five," Joe put in.

"Right," Kara said. "Tune it to that."

Cortez looked from Kara to Dash and for a moment all was still, just the rattle of rotors as the copters closed in. Then he nodded to the radio operator. "Do as she says."

The young woman twisted a dial and speakers crackled. She handed Kara a handset.

302

"Calling The Five," Kara said. "Come in if you can hear me. I have something of yours."

The speakers hissed with static, then a strained voice came on the line. "Kara." She couldn't tell which of them it was, but she assumed Grey. "What have you done with our brother?"

"I'm safe," Dash said, leaning forward.

"And he'll stay that way as long as you do as we tell you," Kara said.

There was a growl of fury and a second voice broke in. "You treacherous—"

"Call off the copters," Kara snapped. "Let the Mariner ships leave."

"We refuse to retreat," Scar said. "We've come too far. The city is ours."

"We know," Kara told him. "Please, just stop the bombing."

"Right now," Joe urged as the flying machines clattered closer, almost overhead. He clung to Kara, ducking his head as they passed within metres of the Ark. But the missiles didn't detach, and through the speakers Kara heard Knuckles barking orders as the copters peeled away.

"You've wounded us, Kara," Grey said.

"We trusted you and you tore us apart," Boxer spat.

"But I warn you," Scar finished, "if anyone so much as lays a hand on our brother, we'll—"

Cortez reached out, cutting the transmission. Then he turned on Dash, fixing him with a hard stare. "I'll do as Kara promised, provided your brothers keep their word. But I warn you, set one foot out of line…"

Kara shoved past him, taking Dash's arm. "He's my hostage, not yours. So leave him be."

She led the clone away, joining the crowd of homeless Mariners huddled on the windblown deck. They stood at the railing, looking back towards the city. Black smoke hung over Frisco Bay.

"You'll see them again, I promise," Kara told him. "And I really am sorry about kidnapping you. It was the sort of thing Cortez would have done. Or your brother, Scar."

Dash smiled, touching his eyebrow. "That's what you call him? It's funny, I always looked up to him. He was so certain about everything. So tough, like nothing could get through."

Kara frowned. "Sometimes I worry that's what I'm like, too."

Dash snorted. "That's ridiculous. My brother always had a mean streak. I'd say you're more like me."

Kara looked down into the glittering water. "Maybe

304

I'm a bit of both."

They passed under the bolted span of the Golden Gate Bridge, moving out into the open ocean. There weren't as many Mariner vessels as she'd hoped and most of them were barely more than fishing boats, swinging in to join the *Neptune* and the *Poseidon*, taking advantage of the big ships' protection. Others were still leaving port, trailing behind them in a ragtag line.

"We're heading north-west," Lynx said, joining them at the railing.

"I wonder where we'll end up," Dash said.

"It's up to Cortez," Kara frowned. "I still can't believe he's back in charge after everything."

"Wherever we're going," Joe put in, "someone'll probably blow it up just after we get there." He looked up at her, his face streaked with soot and tears. "I'm sorry. I know I'd usually say something hopeful right now, but I don't have anything. I just wish Cane was here. And Nate too."

Kara put her arm around his shoulders, bending to kiss his scruffy scalp. "I'm here," she reminded him. "We're alive, and we're back together. Is that hopeful enough for you?"

Joe sighed, forcing a smile. "It's a start."

Epilogue

Nate clutched tight to his aunt's arm as they were shoved along a bombed-out street between rows of high-sided trucks. The Five's train car stood at the far end, the door open, light streaming from within. Their army had crossed the Bay just hours before, half of them coming around by the Golden Gate Bridge while the rest were ferried over on stolen ships. Resistance in the city had been half-hearted and short-lived. The clones now controlled Frisco.

One of them looked up as Nate and Sedna were shown inside; the one with the grey flecks in his hair. He looked weary and disturbed, his face drawn and pale. "Councillor Weaver," he said. "It's good to finally meet you. We are The Five."

Sedna stuck out her chin. "I only count four."

306

Another clone got to his feet, his face bandaged, the scar shining above his eye. "You're not the first to make that observation. You don't want to know what happened to the others."

"Our brother has been taken," a third growled. "If anything happens to him, this city will pay for it."

"Brothers, please," Grey said. "Let's not start this again. The councillor is the highest-ranking member of the Mariner government still in Frisco. We're going to need her help maintaining order."

"Stuff your help," Sedna spat. "You've killed or exiled half my friends. I won't help you oppress the other half."

The fourth clone cracked his knuckles. "We're not planning to oppress them. We just don't want anyone else getting hurt."

"Is that a threat?" Sedna demanded. "Is that why you brought my nephew along, so you could use him to threaten me?"

"Actually, no," Grey said. "We wanted to speak to Nate as well. You'll be glad to hear that your friends are safe. The *Neptune* crossed the thirty-fifth parallel less than an hour ago."

"Th-thank you," Nate said, unsure how else to respond.

"However," Grey went on, leaning closer. "We know the Mariners will be back. John Cortez is not the sort of man to run from a fight, and there's nothing to stop him rallying the rest of the fleet and returning to retake the city. We understand you were with him shortly before he left. We'd like to know what he said to you, anything that could help us predict what he might do next."

"How would my nephew know what goes on in that man's mind?" Sedna demanded. "John Cortez is a disgrace to the Mariner nation – that's why we locked him up."

Nate thought back to that desperate flight through the crowd. He remembered Cane lying twisted on the platform, Cortez swearing bitter revenge. Then Rex had unexpectedly agreed with Joe. He'd told Cortez that—

"Plan B," he remembered aloud. "That's what Rex said, Cortez's brother. After Cane died, everything went crazy. Cortez was screaming, saying he'd kill you. But then his brother calmed him down. He said there was another way to get revenge. Plan B."

Scar rolled his eyes. "Well that's specific."

"Did they say anything else?" Grey asked. "Anything that could give some hint as to what this Plan B entailed?"

"Yes," Nate said. "Rex's exact words were, *Remember Plan B. Remember the transition zone.*"

Sedna's hand tightened on his arm. "Neptune's beard," she said softly. "They're insane."

Grey looked at her quizzically. "What does it mean? What is this zone? How will Cortez use it against us?"

Sedna shook her head. "He won't. I mean, not in the way you think. He's not just going to take revenge on you. He's going to take it on everyone. Everyone who isn't a Mariner. He's going to wash this world clean and start from scratch. He's going to destroy *everything*."

On the DustRoad

Kara, Joe and Nate's journey across the Southern states was inspired by a series of unforgettable road trips, and many of the places they visit are based on real locations.

The Five have their headquarters at the Rothko Chapel in Houston, while the space shuttle Joe sees on the shoreline can be found at the Johnson Space Centre.

The Very Large Array in New Mexico is one of the most breathtaking places on earth, as is Coronado Butte on the rim of the Grand Canyon.

Lenny's pictures are a tribute to the work of Leonard Knight at Salvation Mountain, while the junk maze was loosely inspired by the beaches of the Salton Sea.

The city in the sand is obviously Las Vegas, with Camp Badwater on the western (aka the wrong) side of Death Valley.

I've taken similar liberties with Alcatraz Island and other locations in and around San Francisco because this is the future and a lot has changed.

Thanks and praise to Tom Hughes for thousands of miles of heroic driving, and I'm still sorry about the hot syrup incident. Thanks also to Miles Johnson, Monika Blackburn and many others for hosting and hangs.

Acknowledgements

Kirsty Stansfield steered me round the plot-hole potholes. Ella Diamond Kahn kept the whole show on the road. Jensine Eckwall made another gorgeous map, Manuel Sumberac crafted an even more eye-scorching cover and Elisabetta Barbazza wrestled it all together. The team at Nosy Crow could not have been more supportive, but extra thanks go to Rebecca Mason who has talked me down from a panic more times than is reasonable.

Katia Wengraf was the best indie tour guide ever. So Mayer gave the most sensitive of sensitivity reads. And belated thanks to Drew Worthley for a smashing author pic. My family's enthusiasm and encouragement never wavers – love to Daisy, Alfie, Sarah, Dad, Sadé and Margie, who enables me to visit the real FloodWorld.

Everyone I thanked last time deserves it again (especially if you took the time to shout about *FloodWorld* online). The reaction was better than I could've hoped, but most rewarding of all was meeting young readers and hearing from parents, librarians and teachers who were sharing the book with their classes. Thanks for getting in touch, it means the world.